Lucky whinnied and reared up, eyes rolling in his head as he pulled his lead right out of Ivy's hand.

Ivy staggered back and tripped, only just managing to roll out of the path of his trampling hooves as he bolted. She shouted, 'Lucky, wait!' as he galloped towards the stable door.

She scrambled to her feet, pain shooting through her ankle, only to see Lucky streaking across the ranch, towards the trees.

'What have I done?' she cried.

Sink your fangs into these:

MY SISTER THE VAMPIRE

Switched

Fangtastic!

Revamped!

Vampalicious

Take Two

Love Bites

Lucky Break

Star Style

Twin Spins!

Date with Destiny

Flying Solo

Stake Out!

Double Disaster!

Flipping Out!

Secrets and Spies

Fashion Frightmare!

MY BROTHER THE WEREWOLF

Cry Wolf!

Puppy Love!

Howl-oween!

Tail Spin

Sienna Mercer

MY SISTER THE VAMPIRE

LUCKY BREAK

EGMONT

With special thanks to Sara O'Connor

For all the wacky penguins at WP:
past, present and future

EGMONT
We bring stories to life

My Sister the Vampire: Lucky Break first published in Great Britain 2011
by Egmont UK Limited
The Yellow Building, 1 Nicholas Road, London W11 4AN

ISBN 978 1 4052 5699 5

5 7 9 10 8 6 4

A CIP catalogue record for this title is available from the British Library

Typeset by Avon DataSet Ltd, Bidford on Avon, Warwickshire
Printed and bound by CPI Group (UK) Ltd, Croydon, CR0 4YY

47584/6

EGMONT LUCKY COIN

Our story began over a century ago, when seventeen-year-old
Egmont Harald Petersen found a coin in the street.

He was on his way to buy a flyswatter, a small hand-operated
printing machine that he then set up in his tiny apartment.

The coin brought him such good luck that today Egmont has
offices in over 30 countries around the world. And that lucky
coin is still kept at the company's head offices in Denmark.

Chapter One

Olivia Abbott smiled to herself; the lilac crocuses in the flower beds along the sidewalk were the exact same shade as her mini dress. Franklin Grove was finally shaking off the snow from winter and spring was in the air.

Her twin sister, Ivy Vega, in her stompy black boots, seemed more interested in balancing along the line of black tar that ran between the slabs of concrete than in looking at the flowers.

'Where's he taking us?' Olivia whispered to Ivy.

Mr Vega, their biological dad, was striding a few paces ahead of his daughters like he was being stalked by a vampire hunter. He had asked for another bio-family afternoon together but hadn't told them why.

'Somewhere dark and quiet, I hope,' Ivy whispered back, shading her black-lined eyes with her pale hand. 'All this sunshine is giving me a headache.'

'Don't be such a hermit, Ivy,' Olivia teased. Despite being complete opposites, Olivia totally loved her goth twin.

'Come on, girls,' said Mr Vega, his black blazer flapping as he beckoned them. 'Our table at Mister Smoothie is booked for noon.'

Ivy stumbled, sending her long brown hair flying. 'What?'

Olivia was surprised, too. 'But last time . . .' Last time, Mr Vega had accidentally ordered one of the smoothies that came with a sing-along from the whole restaurant, which hadn't bothered Olivia. But it was just about any self-respecting vampire's worst nightmare and Mr Vega had been mortified.

'Oh, that was only a bit of fun,' Mr Vega said, clearing his throat and looking away.

'Zombie alert!' Ivy called, pretending to be scared. 'Zombies have taken over the town!'

'Don't be silly, Ivy,' Mr Vega said.

'You must be a zombie,' she retorted. 'My father would never willingly go back to the bunniest place in town – no offence, Olivia.'

Olivia didn't take any. All the vampires in Franklin Grove, like Ivy and Mr Vega, called non-vampires, like her, 'bunnies'.

'Don't be silly,' Mr Vega muttered. 'It wasn't that bad.'

What could possibly convince him to go back to Mr Smoothie? Olivia thought. It might not be zombies, but something was going on. There was something both sisters had been wondering about for a few weeks. At the beginning of the year, Mr Vega had told them that he was going to Dallas on a business trip, but Ivy had seen the tag on his suitcase for LAX – Los Angeles airport. Olivia had no idea why he would keep a secret like that.

'You!' commanded a voice.

Olivia looked over to see a woman in a deep purple skirt suit with brown high-heeled boots holding a phone to her ear and pointing straight at her.

It was Amy Teller, movie agent to the most famous male movie star, Jackson Caulfield, who also happened to be Olivia's boyfriend. She marched over, stopping Mr Vega in his tracks.

'No, I didn't mean you. I've already told you!' she shouted into her phone. 'Jackson Caulfield does not do animal costumes.' She clicked the phone shut and pointed at Olivia again. 'You can help me.'

Olivia gulped. 'Uh, sure. What do you need?'

'I need a decent coffee shop,' Amy snapped.

'I think the Meat and Greet serves coffee,' Olivia replied. She was more of a fruit juice kind of girl.

A chirping came from Amy's bag. She pulled out a different phone, checked the screen and then dropped the phone back in her bag, obviously deciding that whoever was calling wasn't worth talking to. 'But do they do a soy latte?' she demanded.

Ivy snorted. 'Doubt it.'

The Meat and Greet was secretly a vampire establishment catering to carnivores. Olivia could get a decent salad there but the word 'soy' was nowhere on their menu.

Something started vibrating in Amy's bag and

she pulled out a third phone. 'I have to take this.' She turned her back on them and started to pace. 'George, darling!' she cooed.

'We need to get going,' Mr Vega told Olivia. 'I, ah, I don't want to lose our favourite booth!'

The perkiness that Mr Vega was putting on made Olivia even more suspicious. He was more of a moody violin than a chipper trumpet, so something was definitely going on.

'OK.' Olivia motioned for Amy to follow them down the sidewalk.

Soon the neon Mister Smoothie sign flashing 'Fruitastic!' came into view and as they crossed the parking lot, Mr Vega seemed to be staring at everyone. Amy was trilling in a high-pitched giggle to whoever George was and Ivy was still muttering about zombies.

Today is turning out to be a strange day, Olivia thought.

'Ciao, darling,' Amy said and rounded on Olivia. 'It's your fault I'm stuck in this tiny one-horse town. The least you could do is help me find a decent cup of coffee.'

Amy was right. Jackson and his family had wanted to get out of Hollywood, and Jackson had convinced them that Franklin Grove was the place to go, because of the good school and quiet lifestyle.

The thought made Olivia want to skip the rest of the way.

'Madam,' Mr Vega put in. 'There are many delightful things hidden in our little town.'

'If you can't *find* a delight,' Amy replied, 'how can it be *delightful*?'

'Why don't you try a smoothie?' Mr Vega said.

Olivia was astounded. Mr Vega had become a Mister Smoothie spokesperson!

'Never mind,' Amy said. 'Just tell me where

Jackson is.'

Olivia shrugged. 'I think he's with Brendan.'

'And who's Brendan?'

'He's my boyfriend,' Ivy put in.

Amy narrowed her eyes. 'And what exactly are they doing?'

'Just hanging out, I guess,' Olivia replied.

'Jackson does not just hang out.' She looked Ivy up and down, taking in her black combat trousers and skull-and-crossbones T-shirt. 'If he goes goth, I will never forgive you. He's already turned down a new big-budget movie series called *Striker*.'

'He did?'

'It would have taken him to St Petersburg for the summer,' Amy went on. 'But instead he wants to audition for the school play of *Romeo and Juliet*. The *school play*!'

Olivia grinned as Amy stalked off, exasperated.

'That woman needs a vacation,' Mr Vega said as they pushed open the door and stepped inside the brightly coloured restaurant.

The three of them approached the counter. Olivia already knew what she wanted, but Ivy buried her nose in the menu.

'I'm pleased to hear your school is putting on *Romeo and Juliet*,' Mr Vega said.

'Me, too,' Olivia said. She was planning to try out for the role of Juliet.

'But, soft! What light through yonder window breaks?' Mr Vega said, putting one hand on his heart and the other pointing towards an imaginary balcony. 'I played Romeo once or twice in my youth.'

'Do you mean what neon horror assaults mine eyes?' Ivy asked.

'I would never be so rude.' Mr Vega smiled.

The serving girl – it was the same one as

on the last visit, Olivia recognised her cow-shaped earrings – looked baffled at their return. 'Welcome to Mister Smoothie?' It was more a question than the usual perky statement. 'I'll be your elixir mixer.'

'I'd like a small Cookies and Cream,' Ivy said.

'And I'll have a Mini-Mommy Pear Perk-Me-Up,' Olivia said.

Mr Vega studied the menu intently.

'How about a Twist and –' Ivy began with a wicked grin on her face. It was the Twist and Shout that made everybody sing.

'No!' Mr Vega jumped in. He cleared his throat. 'I . . . I would like this one.' He pointed to a Spacey Sour Apple smoothie and the serving girl looked relieved.

'Coming right up!' She busied herself with the blender.

'Ah, Shakespeare.' Mr Vega looked wistful

for a moment. Then he grabbed an orange straw from a cow-shaped dispenser. *'En garde!'* he declared, pointing the small plastic 'sword' at Olivia. 'You know, girls, I had to learn stage fighting for the role.'

Then he started to demonstrate by attacking Olivia.

'Hey! You're attacking a defenceless girl!' Olivia shouted. She grabbed a yellow straw in one hand and a pink one in the other.

'O happy dagger!' she declared. It was one of Juliet's lines from the very last scene of the play.

'Touché!' replied Mr Vega and they pretended to duel.

They even did a fun slow motion scene where Mr Vega pretended to get skewered.

'Trips to Mister Smoothie are always eventful,' Ivy said drily as the server handed over the three colourful smoothies.

Olivia poked her tongue out at her sister and followed her over to a four-seater booth by the window with a bunch of mini helium balloons that spelled out 'reserved'. She was impressed with how spontaneous and relaxed her bio-dad was being.

'I'm planning to audition for Juliet,' she said to Mr Vega. She wasn't going to admit it to her bio-dad, but she desperately wanted to play Juliet to Jackson's Romeo.

It would be the most romantic thing, Olivia thought, *to have our first kiss on stage in the most famous love story ever told*. Olivia didn't mind that they hadn't kissed yet. She totally believed in waiting for the right time, and the play could be the perfect moment.

Mr Vega bowed. 'I look forward to watching you from the front row.'

'Uh . . . great!' Olivia made a mental note

that if she did win the part, she would have to bribe an usher to make sure neither of her dads was sitting in the front row. She definitely didn't want them that close if she was going to be kissing Jackson. 'Ivy is going to be the stage manager,' she said to change the subject. 'And my friend Camilla is the director. Although she did say she had some sort of twist planned.'

'A twist in *Romeo and Juliet*?' Mr Vega asked. 'I'm not sure I like the sound of that.'

'Did somebody say *twist* and shout?' Ivy said innocently.

'No!' shouted Mr Vega and Olivia at the same time.

🦇　　　🦇　　　🦇

As Mr Vega sipped his smoothie, Ivy watched him carefully. *Why has he brought us back to Mister Smoothie?*

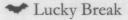

'How's your drink?' she asked.

Mr Vega forced a smile. 'Ah, it is terrific.'

Now I know *something is up*, Ivy thought. *Dad never says terrific. Tragic, tortuous, traumatic . . . but never terrific.*

She didn't know how to pry it out of him. Maybe Olivia had a plan? She nudged her sister's foot. Mr Vega was staring out of the window, so Olivia mouthed, 'What?'

Ivy motioned with her eyes towards their dad. Olivia looked confused. Ivy jerked her head more forcefully but Olivia just shrugged, not understanding.

So much for twin intuition, Ivy thought.

'Hey,' Ivy started at the same time as Olivia said, 'Well,' and Mr Vega began, 'Girls.'

'You go,' Olivia and Ivy said in unison to their dad.

Mr Vega sighed. 'I have something to tell you.'

Here it comes, Ivy thought. *At least I didn't have to torture it out of him.*

'Do you remember when I went on that business trip to Dallas?' he asked.

Olivia nodded, wanting to keep up the pretence, but Ivy blurted, 'You didn't go to Dallas.'

Mr Vega was just about to take a sip of his drink, but the cup slipped between his fingers and he fumbled to catch the smoothie before it spilled over the table. He carefully put the drink down and stared at Ivy. 'How did you know?'

'I saw your luggage tag,' Ivy confessed. 'It said LAX.'

He nodded. 'Indeed, I went to Los Angeles.'

Olivia looked relieved that their bio-dad was finally coming clean.

'What possible reason could you have to

go to one of the sunniest places on earth?' Ivy asked. None of it made sense. Mr Vega's secret trip to LA, all this relaxed chatting and laughing, suggesting a trip here in the first place . . . Ivy much preferred the dad who hung heavy velvet drapes to keep the house cool and dark.

'I was on a mission,' he said. 'I know how important family is to you both.'

Ivy looked at her sister. She had only met her twin at the beginning of the school year and it had taken ages to work out who their real parents were. Once they had realised Ivy's adoptive dad was actually their real dad, they had convinced him to take them on a trip to Transylvania to meet their vampire relatives. It had been so amazing to meet their grandparents, the Count and Countess.

'Having access to your . . . Transylvanian . . .

16

family was relatively easy.' The three of them had just spent a week in their grandparents' goth-gorgeous mansion. 'But I thought it was important for you to connect with the other side of your family too.'

Olivia gasped. 'Our mother's?'

Ivy's mind was reeling. All she'd known about her mother's family was that they lived in a place with big trees, called Owl Creek. She'd always wanted to know more. 'Is that why you were in Los Angeles? I can't keep up. I didn't know our mom had any family in LA,' Ivy said.

'She doesn't.' A female voice made all three of them jump.

Ivy looked up to see an oddly familiar-looking woman, about her dad's age, with soft brown curls and blue eyes. She was slim and wearing faded blue jeans and a fitted red-checked shirt.

She looks like she strolled in right off the farm, Ivy

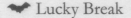

thought. *So why do I think I've seen her before?*

Mr Vega stood up abruptly, knocking over the orange napkin holder. 'I'm so glad you could make it.' The woman didn't make any move to shake his hand. She just stared down at Ivy and Olivia. 'But you're early,' Mr Vega whispered.

'Gosh, Charlie,' she said out loud, looking down at her watch. 'Seven minutes is barely early!'

Charlie!? Ivy thought. No one called her dad Charlie. Well, no one got away with doing it. *Why hasn't he corrected her?*

His cheeks were colouring and Ivy could see that he was stopping himself from saying anything.

'Besides,' the woman went on in her soft southern drawl, 'I'm not going to stand on the street – there's a crazy woman shouting on her cell phone.'

'I was just going to tell the girls about you,' Mr Vega said, fumbling to fit the napkins back into the holder. 'If you'd given me a little more time . . .'

'Well, now you don't have to tell them!' the woman said brightly. 'They can see me for themselves.' She smiled, but the smile didn't travel all the way to her eyes – she seemed nervous.

Olivia looked like she'd been forced to join a rival cheerleading squad and didn't know any of the moves.

Just what is going on? Ivy had only felt this odd sensation once before, when she had come face to face with her twin sister for the first time.

Mr Vega turned to his daughters. 'I'd hoped to prepare you better for this moment. But seeing as she is already here . . . Girls, I would like you to meet your Aunt Rebecca.'

Ivy finally understood. The reason this woman

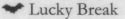

looked so familiar was because she looked *just like* their biological mother.

Olivia gasped. 'You're our mom's sister.'

'Not just her sister.' Rebecca paused and looked from Ivy to Olivia. 'Her twin sister.'

Chapter Two

'That's me,' said Aunt Rebecca, smiling warmly. 'And you two are the spitting image of your mother.'

She was older, obviously, than the photo they'd seen of their mom and her hairstyle was different – but there was no denying it. She looked just like their mother, the same mischievous smile, the same oval chin. Ivy was so surprised, she couldn't think of anything to say.

'I didn't know she was a twin,' Olivia said, grabbing Ivy's hand under the table.

A few months ago, when Ivy learned that their

mother had died in childbirth, it had felt hollow, like something was missing. Aunt Rebecca was the closest she would ever get to her real mom, and she couldn't get closer than a twin. Ivy squeezed Olivia's hand back.

'I wish you'd known about me,' said Aunt Rebecca, casting a glance at Mr Vega. 'And that I'd known about you.'

Uh oh. Ivy realised that there was some tension between the two adults. *That's why he brought us to Mr Smoothie: the First Law of the Night.* No humans could ever know that vampires existed – Olivia being a rare exception – so Mr Vega had to be extra careful that Rebecca didn't get any hint of the truth. You couldn't get more un-vampire than neon lights and cow-shaped straw dispensers.

And Ivy guessed that was why Mr Vega never told Rebecca about the twins and separating them.

Ivy jumped in to try to break the tension.

'Well, it's good to meet you now.'

Mr Vega started to explain, 'I knew she used to live in LA, but –'

'But I moved years ago,' Rebecca interrupted. 'Now, can I give you both a hug?'

Ivy nodded and the twins stood up at the same time. Their aunt smelled like hay and coffee and hugged like a warm, comfy quilt. Ivy wondered if that's what her mom's hug would have felt like.

'Once I realised I was in the wrong place –' Mr Vega started but Rebecca cut him off again.

'I want to know everything about you two,' she said, her eyes glistening as she sat down in the booth next to Mr Vega, but with a distance between them. 'Tell me the whole story!'

'Well,' Olivia began, 'I moved with my parents – my adoptive parents – to Franklin Grove at the beginning of this school year and couldn't believe it when I met Ivy.'

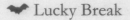

'I bet!' Rebecca said.

'We were completely different but loved each other right away,' Olivia went on. 'It turned out to be quite useful having a twin at times.'

Aunt Rebecca's eyes twinkled.

I wonder if she and our mom got up to some good tricks switching, Ivy thought.

Twin swaps were one of the best parts of being a twin. 'I bet you've got some great stories to tell us about our mom,' Ivy said.

'I sure do,' Rebecca said gently. 'And I'll exchange them for thirteen years of your stories.' Her glance flickered over to Mr Vega, who had folded his arms and was frowning.

Ivy could tell that Rebecca was taking swipes at their dad, but that wasn't fair. He had good reasons for doing what he did – he thought that humans and vampires being together only led to disaster, so he separated his daughters in order

24

to protect them. Even though they could never explain this to Aunt Rebecca, Ivy and Olivia understood and Rebecca shouldn't judge him for doing the best he could.

'Dad,' Ivy said, deliberately giving him a chance to speak. 'How did you find Aunt Rebecca once you found out she'd moved?'

'Well, I couldn't give up at the first obstacle,' he said, clearly pleased to have a chance to change the subject. 'So I did a little asking around in the building. Eventually one of her neighbours told me she'd moved back to –'

'I've been in Beldrake for the past six years,' Rebecca said, holding the smoothie menu in her hand, but not actually looking at it. 'At the ranch where your mom and I spent our summers as kids.'

Ivy could see that her father was struggling not to look annoyed at constantly being talked

25

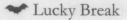

over. *After all*, Ivy thought, *he has gone out of his way to track Aunt Rebecca down.*

'Beldrake is really nearby!' Olivia exclaimed. 'It's less than half an hour away.'

Rebecca nodded. 'I missed life with horses when I was in LA, and when I heard that the ranch was up for sale, I couldn't resist.'

'Would you like a drink, Rebecca?' Mr Vega asked, standing up, but she waved him off. 'I'll just grab some cookies for all of us, then.' He shuffled back to the counter.

'Even though I couldn't afford it, I had to buy it.' She tossed her curly hair. 'That ranch meant so much to me and to your mom. Your mom's favourite horse is still there, you know – his name is Lucky.'

Olivia looked so happy that Ivy wondered if she was going to break into a cheer. 'That's so exciting!' she declared.

Ivy wasn't as enthusiastic. She'd never really had a way with animals. The only pet she'd ever owned, a white-and-tan hamster named Spotty, had run away at every opportunity. She hoped the horses wouldn't turn out to be giant versions of Spotty.

Aunt Rebecca clapped her hands together. 'Oh gosh, I've just had the best idea. You should come to stay next weekend!'

Mr Vega, returning to the table, almost dropped the plate of cookies. 'We were going to discuss this, Rebecca. I haven't had a chance to ask the girls yet if they want to.'

'Well, girls,' she said, her eyes shining. 'Do you want to? I'd love to get to know you and I do need a little help around the ranch.'

Ivy felt bad for her dad, but she did want to see a place from her mom's childhood – and to hear Aunt Rebecca's stories.

'Oh yes, please!' Olivia said. 'I'll have to check with my parents, though.'

'I wouldn't mind,' Ivy admitted.

'I will allow it,' Mr Vega said, softening, 'as long as your homework is done and it doesn't interfere with Olivia's audition.'

'Oooh!' Rebecca squealed, full of enthusiasm. Ivy wondered if Olivia would look like her when she grew up. 'Auditions! What for?'

'I'm trying out to be Juliet,' Olivia said, a little shy to tell her. 'But the auditions are on Monday, so it wouldn't interfere.'

'Oh, I love *Romeo and Juliet*!' Aunt Rebecca clapped her hands together. 'You can do lots of rehearsing on the ranch once you get the part; it's so peaceful. And I'll make sure you've got time for homework. Oh, this will be so much fun!'

Mr Vega sighed.

Olivia beamed.

Ivy jumped as someone tapped on the window.

Then she grinned as she realised the black hair and beautiful smile belonged to her boyfriend, Brendan Daniels. He crossed his eyes and made a silly face, so Ivy stuck her tongue out at him. Then he waved at everyone else at the table.

'Who is that?' Rebecca frowned. 'Should I call security?'

'No, no!' Mr Vega chuckled. 'That is Ivy's boyfriend.'

'Oh,' said Rebecca, her face not really changing. 'Isn't that trench coat too warm? Why would anyone want to wear all black on a sunny day like today?'

'Ahem.' Ivy cleared her throat. She was wearing all black and so was her dad. She hoped her aunt wasn't the kind of person to judge people on how they dressed.

Outside, Brendan beckoned someone over.

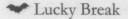

Jackson appeared at the window, waving to Olivia.

'Oh, I know him!' Rebecca declared. 'Isn't he a famous movie star?'

Olivia nodded. 'He's my boyfriend. And he's trying out for Romeo.'

'Wow!' Rebecca said. 'I wish I'd dated a movie star when I was your age.'

Brendan mouthed, 'See you later.' Then the boys headed away, towards the mall.

A moment after the boys disappeared around the corner, Ivy spotted Amy Teller stalking them like a secret agent.

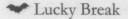

'And Romeo leap to these arms, untalk'd of and unseen.'

Olivia didn't usually chew her fingernails – but she desperately wanted her Juliet audition to go well, and her nails had taken the brunt of her nervousness. All during her Monday classes it was on her mind, and the instant that the final bell had rung, she'd rushed to the theatre to get ready – along with what seemed like the whole school.

Now, she was sitting in front of one of the lighted mirrors in the girls' dressing room, applying a fresh coat of lip gloss and running through her lines.

'Excuse me,' said Charlotte Brown, wearing thick red rouge on her cheeks and a pseudo-Elizabethan dress. 'Can I share your mirror?' Without even waiting for an answer, Charlotte had leant in so close to apply eyeliner that all Olivia could see was Charlotte's rear end.

Olivia sighed. Charlotte was both the captain of the cheerleading squad and the least considerate person Olivia knew.

'You wouldn't mind if I kissed your boyfriend,

would you?' Charlotte said, not even turning around.

Olivia almost dropped her lip gloss. 'What?'

'Well,' she said, 'when I'm Juliet, I'll have to kiss Romeo, and everyone knows Jackson is a shoo-in for the part.'

'Let's just see what happens,' Olivia replied, trying to avoid a conflict.

There is no way Charlotte Brown will be kissing my boyfriend . . . before I get to! She stood up to find a quieter place to finish running through her lines. She had to get this audition right – and not just because of Charlotte. Playing opposite Jackson as Romeo would be so romantic.

'Could you scoot over?' Charlotte whined.

Olivia left the dressing room and walked into the huge backstage space that had tons of props from previous productions, like a giant tree that a person could fit into, from the musical *Into the Woods*.

Olivia pushed her way past a group of girls doing vocal exercises to sit down on a Victorian sofa from *The Importance of Being Earnest* and started from the top. Out of the corner of her eye, Olivia spotted Jackson in a quiet corner on the other side of the big backstage space, sitting on a wooden cube and reading his audition scene to himself.

Like he even needs to try, Olivia thought. There was no way Camilla could cast anyone else as Romeo. He was just so . . . so perfect! It made her like him even more that he was taking it so seriously. Other movie stars would probably not even try.

She closed her eyes and imagined what it would be like – her hair would be tumbling over her shoulders, and she'd have on some gorgeous golden gown. Jackson would wear a flowing white shirt and sweep her up in his arms, reciting beautiful poetry. Lost in the emotion of the passionate love story, he would look deep into her eyes, lean in and –

'Oof!' said a gruff voice as someone knocked into Olivia's sofa.

'Hey!' Olivia's eyes flew open to see Garrick Stevens, the greasiest of the four Beasts, staring right in her face.

Ugh, she thought. *That's the fastest way to ruin a romantic daydream.*

Garrick was a vampire and he trooped around school with his three vampire friends in a pack. They called themselves the Beasts. He continually risked breaking the First Law through sheer stupidity. He'd even tried to bite a cheerleader once but had chickened out at the last minute.

'Huh, huh.' His laugh sounded like spinning helicopter blades. 'Sorry, Olivia.' He grinned. 'Or should I say, I beggeth your pardon, my Juliet?'

'*You're* auditioning for Romeo?' Olivia asked incredulously.

'Yeah,' he said, like she'd just asked him if coffins creaked. 'There's, like, five kissing scenes.'

Olivia crinkled her nose. 'Well, good luck.'

'I'm making my own luck,' Garrick said and grinned wickedly. Then he sauntered off towards Jackson.

Whatever, Olivia thought. *There is no way Garrick could possibly be Romeo.*

'Hey, sis!' Ivy appeared out of nowhere, her all-black turtleneck blending in with the black curtains. Her only concession to the warmer spring weather was to wear a knee-length skirt with her boots, rather than a floor-length one. 'You ready?' She had on headphones with a microphone attached and was holding a clipboard – in full-on stage-manager mode. 'The director is on her way.'

'As ready as I'll ever be,' Olivia said.

'Five minutes to start, folks,' Ivy said to anyone within earshot, making Olivia's stomach do a handspring. 'I hope you've paid attention to the auditioning order. If you miss your slot, you're out of luck.'

A younger girl with red hair looked terrified at Ivy's firm tone and Olivia gave her a reassuring smile. 'Don't worry,' she said. 'Just don't go somewhere to fix your hair before your turn.'

The girl didn't look any more relaxed.

Ivy moved around backstage, giving the little groups of nervous auditionees the same message. Olivia could see Sophia Hewitt, Ivy's best friend and the other half of the backstage team, doing the same. One girl with pigtails rushed towards the backstage bathroom with her hand over her mouth.

Poor girl, Olivia thought.

She glanced over to see what Jackson was doing and saw Ivy walking towards him. With each step, an odd cloud of greenish powder billowed up from around Ivy's feet.

What's powder doing on the ground? Olivia wondered. *That could make people slip!*

An instant later, Ivy let out a yowl. 'A-eeee!' She dropped her clipboard with a clatter and crouched down to scratch furiously at her legs and ankles.

Olivia hurried over, being sure to avoid the powder. 'What's happened?' Jackson was already trying to help hold Ivy up while she balanced awkwardly on one leg.

'Itching!' Ivy shrieked. 'Itching everywhere!'

Olivia took her other arm for support while Sophia rushed over. 'What's going on?' she demanded.

'Eeiii dooooon't knoooooow,' Ivy wailed,

rubbing her legs in desperation.

Jackson bent down to examine the ground.

'Is it fire ants or something?' Olivia asked, struggling to support Ivy, who was half-standing and half-collapsed on to one knee.

'I can't see any,' said Sophia.

'There's your culprit.' Jackson pointed to a paper bag, only half-hidden under a dusty tweed armchair. 'All this green stuff is itching powder.' He pulled the bag out carefully and folded it up, making sure no more powder escaped.

The other auditionees had gathered around.

'Nobody step on that,' Sophia ordered to everyone nearby.

'Grr . . . Arrg!' Now Ivy was sitting down, scrambling to yank off her shoes. 'Scratch my foot!'

Olivia crinkled her nose. That was one of the grossest things she could imagine.

'Um . . . No, thanks.'

'Is she auditioning for a different play?' asked a younger boy, wearing a Robin-Hood-style cap with a feather in it.

'I'll be right back,' Jackson said.

Olivia was left in charge of a convulsing Ivy.

'Scratch my foot!' Ivy screeched again. 'I can't do both at once.'

'Somebody put that cat out of its misery,' sneered Charlotte.

'Shut up,' commanded Sophia.

Charlotte shut her mouth automatically, shocked to have been put in her place.

Olivia took a deep breath, closed her eyes and knelt down to help her sister. Ivy's pale legs were red from all the scratching, and her toes kept curling up with each yelp.

Olivia reached out hesitantly, not sure she could actually do this. 'You so owe me,' she muttered.

She took Ivy's ankle in one hand and was just about to scratch it when Jackson interrupted.

'These should help.' He handed over a stack of wet paper towels.

Just in time, Olivia thought with relief, dropping Ivy's leg and hastily climbing to her feet.

Ivy pressed the damp towels against her legs, closing her eyes with relief, while Sophia and Jackson worked to mop up the powder on the ground. 'Oh my darkness, that's so much better.' Ivy closed her eyes and flopped back on to the wooden floor.

Olivia was baffled. 'Why would anyone go after the stage manager with itching powder?'

'I'm going to guess that it was meant for me,' Jackson said. 'No one else was over here – and I *am* auditioning for the lead. Sorry, Ivy.'

Sophia frowned. 'But why would anyone resort to sabotage?'

Olivia looked around at the actors who were still watching the drama unfold. It was true that anyone who was auditioning for Romeo would see Jackson as their main threat, but this was pretty devious.

'Whoever it was is in for a staking,' Ivy said, finally calming down now that the damp towels had relieved the itching. She gazed down at her ankles. They were red-raw from scratching and an angry rash ran all the way up her legs. Whoever had done this had meant business.

'That is blatant cheating and someone is going to get disqualified from the auditions.' Ivy pointed a long finger at Jackson. 'Hand over that powder!'

'Yes, ma'am,' Jackson said, passing her the little brown bag.

As soon as it was in her hand, she whirled around. 'Did anyone see anything?'

'I didn't,' said the feather-in-cap guy.

'Not me,' replied Sophia.

Out of the corner of her eye, Olivia spotted Garrick disappearing behind a curtain, obviously trying not to be seen.

His voice echoed in her head. 'I'm making my own luck,' he'd said. Itching powder was *exactly* the kind of thing Garrick Stevens would go for.

'Ivy,' Olivia began and Ivy whipped her head around. 'If you promise not to kill the messenger, I think I know who did it.'

'Speak!' she commanded.

Olivia drew her deeper backstage, among the dusty wardrobes filled with props, where most theatre hopefuls wouldn't dare tread.

Jackson and Sophia followed, out of earshot of the rest of the auditionees.

'Garrick Stevens,' Olivia explained. 'I'm pretty sure of it, actually. Garrick was lurking around five minutes ago and he was definitely up to something.'

'He did come over and ask for the number of my dentist, which seemed very odd,' Jackson said.

Olivia rolled her eyes. She wasn't going to explain it to Jackson, but vampires had to get their teeth filed regularly, and Garrick was always trying to find a dentist who would make him a set of false fangs.

Ivy took a closer look at the brown paper bag in her hand. There was a doodle in black felt tip. 'And it doesn't take a secret agent to figure out what that means.' She held the bag out so the others could look.

Olivia saw a tiny B with devil horns scrawled in black pen on the corner of the bag.

'The Beast left his calling card,' said Sophia.

'Garrick is so dead,' Ivy said. 'I don't know how yet, but I will have my revenge.'

Sophia grinned and tapped her headphones. 'If you need help, just call.'

'Alack, there lies more peril in *mine* eye than twenty swords!' Ivy declared.

Olivia's jaw dropped. 'How come *you're* spouting Shakespeare?'

'I'm the stage manager, which means I know the whole script back to front.' Ivy turned back to the auditionees. 'It also means I have less than sixty seconds to get you all out into the auditorium. Move it!'

Ivy had to abandon her socks and shoes, because they were covered in the powder, so she slipped into a pair of bright red clown shoes, with a look on her face that dared anyone to comment.

Everyone, including Olivia and Jackson, scurried to do her bidding. Olivia nearly sprinted through the wings, stage right, and down the side steps to plop into a seat in the third row. Jackson had gone straight through the gap in the main curtain and ended up on the opposite side of the auditorium. There was no way she could talk to him again before the auditions started.

Probably just as well, Olivia thought. She was nervous enough as it was, and having him nearby might completely distract her.

The back doors to the auditorium burst open and in strode Camilla, dressed in a black beret, dark sunglasses and red braces holding up her camouflage trousers. She looked half French director, half army sergeant. She marched down the centre aisle to the edge of the stage. 'OK, people,' Camilla said to the crowd. 'Thank you for coming. Good luck to you all. You have one chance. There will not be callbacks.'

One of the guys behind Olivia muttered, 'She looks tough.'

Olivia was proud of her friend. Usually Camilla had her nose buried in a science-fiction novel, but today she was taking charge.

'I am not your average director and this is not your average production of *Romeo and Juliet*,' she went on. 'We only have three weeks to pull it together, so I want passion; I want originality – I want that something special.' Camilla turned to the stage, settled in the front row, middle seat, took out a clipboard and barked, 'Who's first?'

Ivy was stage left and motioned for the first auditionee to come up on stage. It was Charlotte, smiling demurely, and looking every inch a Juliet in her period dress. It had a frilly-sleeved white top under an embroidered blue dress that flared out at the waist. Charlotte flashed Jackson a huge eyelash-fluttering smile.

Olivia squeezed her eyes shut, willing the

spirit of Shakespeare to write a happy scene and not the tragedy of Charlotte getting to play Jackson's Juliet.

Chapter Three

Ivy looked down at her clipboard. The first three auditions were complete and the next one, Toby Decker, wearing a full tuxedo, was taking his place to read a monologue for Mercutio, the second most important male part.

Her eye fell on a name near the bottom of her list: Garrick Stevens.

Her leg twitched and she had to scratch it, even though the irritation from half an hour ago had pretty much faded. She wondered if her legs would ever forget.

She had secured the little brown bag of

evidence under the metal clip of her clipboard and was planning to show it to Camilla to get Garrick disqualified.

Unless . . . Ivy thought, *there's a better way to punish him . . .*

An idea started forming in her mind.

🦇　　　🦇　　　🦇

Olivia was in the wings, stage right, waiting for her turn and watching Camilla as she scribbled notes on the current auditionee. Her face was like a halfway line — dead straight. Olivia didn't have any clue what she was thinking.

'Next!' called out Ivy and Olivia knew that meant her.

She stood up, adjusted her light-blue maxi dress and strode up on to the stage. She winked at her sister, who gave a little thumbs up back, and went to stand on her mark.

The stage lights were bright, so she couldn't

see much of the auditorium. But that only helped her imagine the scene: standing on a balcony above an orchard filled with apple trees and sunshine, longing for the person she loved.

'I'm performing Juliet's monologue from Act Three, Scene Two,' she said, peering out into the spotlights. Then she forced her mind to clear and began:

'Gallop apace, you fiery-footed steeds, towards Phoebus' lodging . . .'

Olivia had been determined not to let the old-sounding English intimidate her, and she spoke each line carefully and clearly.

'. . . Come, night; come, Romeo; come, thou day in night.'

She'd studied the passage carefully to figure out what each line was trying to say and, now, all she had to do was think of Jackson to feel the romance of Shakespeare's poetry. It felt so natural that she could get lost in the words.

'Give me my Jackson; and, when he shall die . . .'

She heard a couple of giggles and at least one snort from the audience.

Oh no! Olivia thought. *I just said 'Jackson' instead of 'Romeo'!*

She tried to stay in character. *Oh no, oh no, this is bad – don't blush. Don't blush!*

Olivia was sure her face was at least a little rosy – but she forced herself to deliver the rest of the monologue. The spotlights were sending out loads of heat and she could feel her body getting warmer and warmer, but she tried to blank that from her mind and concentrate on the rest of the monologue.

'Take him and cut him out in little stars, and he will make the face of heaven so fine that all the world will be in love with night and pay no worship to the garish sun . . .'

When she reached the end of her piece she gave a small curtsey and the audience clapped enthusiastically.

I think that's more than they did for Charlotte, Olivia hoped. *But is that enough for me to get the part?*

She walked off the stage, trying to read Camilla's face, but she was bent over her clipboard, busy writing something. It almost looked like she was frowning until her friend looked up and gave her a little wink. Olivia's heart leaped.

That has to be good, Olivia thought. *Oh please, oh please, oh please!* Getting this role meant everything to Olivia.

As she made her way back to her seat, she caught sight of Jackson, who was grinning like a Mister Smoothie server. Olivia blushed to herself. The perfect boyfriend, the perfect Romeo. It all just had to add up to the perfect first kiss.

Olivia decided she would go over and sit with him until his audition, but then Ivy called out his name.

She sat down in the nearest seat to watch him at work.

He climbed on to the stage and stood on his mark, looking up towards the top tier of the audience. 'But, soft! What light through yonder window breaks? It is the east, and Juliet is the sun . . .'

Jackson spoke softly, but he held everyone's attention. Camilla was leaning forward in her seat and the muttering audience had fallen utterly silent.

'. . . It is my lady, O, it is my love! O, that she knew she were!'

In front of Olivia two eighth-grade girls were swooning over him. 'I wish he was my Romeo,' said the one that had a red ponytail.

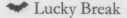

She smiled with the knowledge that he was hers. A few weeks ago, she'd been a bit paranoid about how he felt about her. Now, since his visit to Transylvania, she was sure of Jackson's commitment to her, even if he was an A-list Hollywood dreamboat.

Olivia bit her bottom lip and wished again that she would be cast as Juliet, to play opposite *her* Romeo.

As Jackson said his last line, Ivy unclipped the itching powder. Garrick was up next and she had to be ready to make her move.

I'm going to make sure Garrick's audition is the highlight of the day, she thought. Not because he was a good actor, but because he was going to be doing a very good impression of . . . a person with itching powder down their shirt.

Jackson bowed to thunderous applause,

with a few shrieks as well.

Ivy squinted against the glare of the stage lights and saw that there were definitely more girls in the audience than were auditioning. Some of the girls from school must have snuck in to watch Jackson's audition.

When the noise quietened down, Ivy called out Garrick's name. She unfolded the top corner of the bag, ready to spring when he came close enough.

Garrick leaped out of his seat and his three Beastly friends, Dylan Soyle, Kyle Glass and Ricky Slitherman, started whooping. He looked a little out of place wearing a skull-and-crossbones T-shirt and scruffy black jeans. He hadn't exactly made an effort to be presentable for his audition.

'Garrick is the man!' shouted Dylan.

Garrick leered at the crowd, waving like he

had a hundred fans screaming his name, and sauntered up on stage.

Ivy knew she was going to have approximately one millisecond to accomplish her mission – and she had to be subtle, too. If he spotted the bag, he'd know what she was trying to do.

Garrick was approaching fast.

'Hey, babe,' he said when he was about three steps away. 'Make sure you mark down that I've been on TV before. Jackson's not the only one with on-screen experience.'

Ivy forced herself not to roll her eyes. Garrick had been on TV during a lame stunt where he'd crawled out of a coffin at a funeral – it had been a complete mess that Ivy had had to clean up.

'Why don't you mark it yourself?' she said slyly, holding out her clipboard. 'Right here on my list.'

As Garrick craned over to scrawl 'TV star' beside his name, the back of his T-shirt gaped open. *Perfect.* Ivy didn't waste a second. She tipped the beastly powder right down his collar.

'Thanks, babe,' he said, handing the pen back to her.

'My pleasure,' she said, grinning.

Then he strolled out on to the stage, confidence oozing from his every pore.

Three, two, one.

Garrick froze. His shoulders twitched. His right arm waggled. Ivy smiled.

'Uh, can I do my audition later?' Garrick blurted, doing a little wiggly dance.

'No time outs, no do-overs. It's now or never, Garrick,' said Camilla firmly.

Ivy remembered the agony of itching all over her legs – and she had been able to abandon all dignity and scratch herself. Garrick couldn't melt

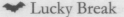

into a frenzy because he was on stage in front of half the school.

Thought you could cheat and sabotage Jackson? Ivy wanted to say. *Not on my watch.*

Garrick glanced over at her, eyes watering, and she waved the bag at him, so he knew exactly what had happened to him.

He started doing a strange little dance, like a four-year-old desperate for the bathroom.

He spluttered out his first line, 'But, but, but, soft?' It sounded more like a plea than a declaration of love.

Ivy hid her face behind her clipboard so that no one could see her giggling.

'Was that you?' came Sophia's voice through her headphones.

'Yup,' she whispered back.

Garrick was doing the same monologue as Jackson. *With a slightly different interpretation,* she thought. Garrick's head jerked from side to side.

'W-w-what light . . .' Twitch. 'Through yonDER.' Hop. 'Window-oh-oh.' Jump. 'Breaks.'

He gave in to the urge to scratch and was lurching about as he said the lines: 'It is the east, and Juliet is the sun!'

Ivy was impressed that he could still remember his lines. He threw himself to the ground and started writhing like a beetle on its back, shouting the lines louder and louder.

'Arise, fair sun, and KILL the envious mooooon . . .'

Ivy caught sight of Olivia sitting in the audience, twitching herself, trying not to laugh out loud.

By now, several people in the audience were sniggering, while Camilla looked utterly shocked.

When Garrick had finally finished his monologue, he fled the stage. He rushed right past Ivy into the wings and she heard the backstage bathroom door slam open. His three cronies ran backstage after him to find out what had happened.

Serves you right, Ivy thought.

'Next!' she shouted.

Half an hour later, Olivia was sitting in the sixth row of the theatre, holding hands with Jackson, waiting to hear the big news.

'It's so going to be me,' Charlotte declared over the excited hubbub of the theatre. She was two rows in front, sitting between Allison and Katie. 'No one else even came close.'

Jackson squeezed Olivia's hand and said quietly, 'Don't listen to her. Your audition was really good.'

Olivia smiled, but her heart fluttered. There was a real possibility that Charlotte would get the part.

Camilla was up in the sound booth, the little room above the back row of the audience, making her decisions in private.

Jackson chuckled. 'I especially liked the part where you were talking about me.'

Olivia's entire body tingled with embarrassment and she hoped she wasn't going redder than a tomato dunked in ketchup. 'I couldn't help it,' she admitted. 'I was thinking of you to try to get the romance across.'

He smiled at her and leaned closer. 'Well, it worked.'

Olivia breathed in. *Is he going to kiss me right now?*

Just then, Ivy plopped down in a seat in front of them, facing backwards.

Jackson straightened up and Olivia let out her breath.

'It won't be long now,' Ivy said, still wearing her headphones. 'I just went up to check with her.'

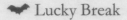

Olivia gasped. 'Did you see anything?'

Ivy shook her head. 'Not a sausage. And I wouldn't tell you anyway. That would compromise my professional integrity.'

'Speaking of professional integrity,' Jackson said, 'I think some of the itching powder evidence might have gone astray.'

Ivy put on an innocent face. 'I don't know what you're talking about.'

The three of them glanced over at Garrick, who was sitting several seats behind them, looking grumpy and hilarious in a red-and-yellow polka-dotted shirt that he'd had to borrow from the costume department.

'I'm surprised he hasn't made a fuss about you, Ivy,' said Olivia.

'If he did,' Ivy replied, 'he would have to admit that he was the person who first brought itching powder into the theatre.'

Olivia heard something crackle in Ivy's headphones.

'She's ready!' Ivy said and hurried up the centre aisle to the back of the auditorium. She held open one of the doors and Camilla appeared, a dark silhouette against the lights in the lobby. The theatre fell completely silent as she came down the steps to the front of the stage, a thumb hooked into one of her red braces.

'In my hand,' she said in an ominous tone, 'I have the final cast list.'

Being a director really suits Camilla, thought Olivia.

She glanced at Jackson, who looked as relaxed as if he was waiting to hear what was in the cafeteria for lunch tomorrow. Olivia felt more like she was about to hear whether or not she was going to *be* lunch tomorrow.

'Thank you all for taking the time to

audition,' Camilla continued, 'and please remember: if you don't get a part, we need lots of support backstage with props and painting sets.'

Olivia glanced around at everyone else in the seats. The girl with the ponytail looked stony-faced and pale, and the boy with the Robin Hood cap looked like he'd won his role already. It was very tense.

Camilla cleared her throat. 'For the female leads, in the role of Juliet, will be . . .'

Olivia squeezed Jackson's hand so hard she made him yelp.

'Olivia Abbott!'

Over the polite applause, Charlotte glared at Olivia. 'No way!'

But Olivia refused to let that dampen her spirits. She squealed and clapped and grabbed Jackson in a huge hug, which was awkward with the arm of the chair between them.

I did it! she thought. *I'm going to play Juliet . . . with Jackson playing Romeo! We will finally have our first kiss.*

The babble died down and Camilla made her next announcement. 'The second female lead, the part of the nurse, will be played by Charlotte Brown.'

'The nurse?' Charlotte whined. 'Isn't she old?'

Camilla ignored her. 'For the male leads, in the role of Mercutio will be . . . Jackson Caulfield.'

'What!' Olivia said. *Jackson didn't even audition for that role*, she thought.

The whole audience murmured their surprise.

'That's great,' Jackson said, without a trace of confusion. 'He's such a complex character.'

Olivia couldn't believe it. Jackson seemed genuinely pleased.

But wait, she thought. *This is ridiculous – he's the*

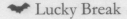

*most famous young movie star in the whole world! How
can he not have gotten the lead?*

Camilla called for quiet, but the audience kept
muttering about who could possibly have the
lead role if Jackson didn't.

*But Jackson is a professional! Who at this school could
possibly have out-acted him?* Olivia wondered.

Suddenly, a shrill whistle pierced the air,
making everyone shut up. 'I said: quiet, please.'
Camilla took her two fingers out of her mouth.
'Thank you. In the role of Romeo, will be . . .
Garrick Stephens.'

'Yessss!' shouted Garrick, leaping out of his seat.

'Double what!' Olivia said. 'Garrick is Romeo?'

'The supporting roles will be posted outside
momentarily.' Camilla had to shout over the
noise of the auditionees – some disappointed at
not getting lead roles but most chattering about
Garrick. 'Will the four leads please stay behind

for a briefing? The rest of you may go.'

Olivia was stunned. Garrick had spent his entire audition twitching and hopping all over the place . . . He was awful! At one point, he was actually *lying down* on the stage! She couldn't make sense of it, but made her way up to the front, following Jackson through the dispersing crowd.

'You might be wondering,' Camilla said when the four of them had gathered around, 'why the roles were cast in this way.'

Olivia held herself back from shouting, 'You bet I am!'

'If you'll follow me, I have something to show you.' She led the small group up the side steps on to the stage. She paused before taking them into the wings. 'You may have heard that my production of *Romeo and Juliet* was going to have a "twist",' she said and the four of them nodded. 'Well –'

Before Camilla could continue, the theatre doors banged open and in strode their stuffy English teacher, Mr Wagenbach, closely followed by Amy Teller. Mr Wagenbach brandished a stack of papers that looked like a script and his face was the same shade of aubergine as his tie.

'H-how could you?' he spluttered as he stomped up the stage steps. 'This so-called "adaptation" of *Romeo and Juliet* is an abomination!'

Olivia was stunned, but Camilla looked completely composed.

'How can you cast the most famous lovers in all of literature as aliens and robots?' he shouted.

Robots? Olivia thought. *What is he talking about?*

'If you would just calm down, sir,' Camilla began.

'I will not calm down, young lady!' he ranted. 'You cannot set one of Shakespeare's most famous plays in outer space! I have a mind to cancel this production with immediate effect.'

It finally hit Olivia – the twist Camilla had been about to reveal was that the play had a sci-fi theme. She truly was making it her own.

Does this mean I have to learn cyborg? Olivia wondered, knowing her friend was fluent in the Cyborg Beta language.

Amy Teller had been nudging closer and closer to Jackson. She straightened her green tailored jacket. 'If you think that Jackson Caulfield is going to waste his time in the lead role of this nonsense, you should think again.'

Camilla narrowed her eyes. 'I'm pleased to inform you that Garrick Stevens will be playing the lead in my play.'

Both adults turned to stare at the lanky, oddly dressed person who, up until then, had been doodling on his jeans in black pen.

He waved, accidentally dropping the pen.

'That's me.' Then he reached over his shoulder to scratch his back.

Amy whipped her head back to Camilla. 'You are kidding me.'

'I get to play Mercutio,' Jackson put in.

Amy gasped. 'But he dies halfway through.'

Jackson turned to Camilla. 'And I have to say thank you for the opportunity. You should know that I am *fully committed* to this production.' He looked at Amy pointedly. 'And all my other engagements will be cancelled until after closing night.'

Amy looked like a goldfish. Her mouth kept opening and closing, with no sound coming out.

Camilla nodded. 'Thank you.' Then she turned to the adults. 'Look, I am aware that Shakespeare in outer space isn't how it's usually done, but that is the best thing about his plays. They are universal, and his stories and characters are so rich they can be brought to life anywhere.'

Mr Wagenbach's purple faded to lilac.

Camilla kept going. 'Changing the setting will open his message to a wider audience, who might not otherwise appreciate the quality of his writing. I want the school – no, the world – to see how powerful it can be.'

Olivia was impressed. Her friend knew exactly what to say to win over the teacher. It was almost a call to arms, an impassioned advertisement for Mr Wagenbach's favourite playwright.

'Perhaps . . .' he began. 'Perhaps you are right.'

Amy Teller rolled her eyes.

'I was hasty in my judgement,' he decided. 'You carry on, Camilla. Our school – and our drama department – is lucky to have someone like you.'

'Thank you,' she said politely.

'I want approval over the costume,' demanded Amy.

Camilla crossed her arms. 'I'm willing to offer consultation, but that's as far as it goes.'

Olivia was impressed with how well Camilla could handle the fireball that was Jackson's manager. *I wouldn't want to have to negotiate with either of them*, Olivia thought.

'Consultation is for D-listers,' Amy retorted. 'Jackson is an A-plus-lister.'

'I have faith in my director, Amy,' Jackson said, stepping to Camilla's defence. 'She has the most invested in this production, and I'm sure everything will look great.'

Amy narrowed her eyes. 'Well, I'm not calling *Inside Hollywood* until I see the costumes.'

As Amy and Mr Wagenbach left the theatre, Camilla turned back to her actors.

Charlotte looked like a balloon about to pop.

'*What* were they talking about?' she demanded.

'That's what I was trying to tell you,' Camilla explained. 'Come with me.' She pushed aside a heavy black curtain and walked through the wings. She opened a side door into the costume room and led the small group to a rack near the back.

'This will be a Coal Knightley-inspired version of *Romeo and Juliet*. The words and the story are pretty much the same, but the Capulets are robots and the Montagues are aliens. It's going to be awesome!'

Garrick looked confused. 'Aliens?'

'Haven't you guys seen that awesome 1950s movie *Forbidden Planet*?' she said enthusiastically. 'It was sci-fi Shakespeare and a total cult phenomenon.'

Olivia shook her head. 'Sorry.' She stared at the metallic outfits and tentacle-like arms that were hanging from the rack. Sci-fi Shakespeare was definitely going to be . . . memorable.

'Garrick, your twitchy audition was even better than I could have imagined for the part of Romeo – or Romezog, as you will be called,' Camilla said.

'Romezog, huh?' Garrick said. 'Will there still be all the kissing?'

'The script isn't changing much from the original,' Camilla confirmed.

'Oh yes!' Garrick punched the air.

'Oh no,' Olivia groaned.

'Congratulations on being Juliet, Olivia,' Charlotte said, smirking.

'Actually, it's Julietron,' Camilla corrected, pulling a short, plastic skirt and stiff sleeveless top off the rack and handing it to Olivia. It looked like a cheerleader's outfit that had been dipped in liquid gold.

Cool, Olivia thought.

'Charlotte, you will be Nanny-bot and wear this.' She handed her a grey wig and a padded, shapeless dress made of silver fabric with pink rose appliqués ironed all over it.

'Blech.' Charlotte turned up her nose.

'And, you, Jackson will be Merc-X88.' She handed him a futuristic-looking knight costume where the helmet had tubes to join it to the breastplate. 'As a relative of the Prince, you're not an alien or a robot.'

'I'm a cyborg,' he said. 'I'm both!'

'Exactly,' Camilla confirmed. She turned to Garrick. 'You will be required to wear this.'

Romezog's costume was green and had four arms on each side that were strung together to move whenever he moved his arms. There was also a hat with big eyes on springs, bouncing all over the place.

'I can handle that,' Garrick said, leering at Olivia. He blew her a kiss.

It turned her stomach.

Today should have been the best day ever. She had actually won the role of Juliet – plus she had a fabulous costume – but she hadn't even considered that Jackson wouldn't get the role of Romeo.

Now, not only was she *not* going to have her first kiss with Jackson while performing the most famous love story in the world – it was going to be with Garrick Stevens . . . dressed as an octopus.

Life couldn't get much worse.

Chapter Four

'What have you got in here?' Brendan asked, pushing his long hair out of his face and hauling Ivy's black duffel bag across the porch towards her dad's car.

It was Saturday morning, after a week of intense rehearsals, and she and Olivia were just about to head off to Aunt Rebecca's farm for the night. Ivy was looking forward to spending time with her aunt but hoping to avoid the four-legged residents of the farm.

'I tried to pack light,' Ivy replied. 'Well, not light colours, of course.'

'And yet you've ended up with a bag that weighs more than a solid marble tombstone,' Brendan said.

'Sorry,' she said and gave him a quick kiss on the cheek. 'I didn't know what to pack for a farm.' She had eventually decided to wear her black and grey camos and a three-quarter sleeve T-shirt. At least she knew her sturdy boots would do the trick. 'Plus I had to pack some Vita-Vamp bars.' If Aunt Rebecca didn't serve much meat, Ivy had to make sure she had enough iron intake. It wasn't easy staying overnight with someone who didn't know about the whole vampire thing.

'I still can't believe you're off to be a cowgirl out in the sticks,' Brendan said.

'Just point me to the cows that need a-milking,' Ivy joked.

'This I have got to see,' he replied, and they dissolved into giggles.

'Come on, you two!' Mr Vega called, using his vampire strength to easily lift Olivia's bag into the back of his car. 'We're leaving in five minutes.'

Olivia and her pink leather overnight bag had just been dropped off by Mr Abbott, who was on his way to a weekend seminar on the discipline of ikebana, Japanese flower arranging.

'To calm the soul,' he had intoned, just before he drove off.

Ivy needed some soul-calming. She was really excited to spend time with her aunt, but she had no idea what to do on a farm. Despite her joking, she really did not want to milk any cows.

'Where is he?' Olivia hopped from one foot to the other, as Brendan and Mr Vega heaved Ivy's bag into the car. 'Jackson said he'd come and say goodbye.'

Just then, a sleek chauffeured car pulled up at the end of the driveway and Jackson jumped out and hurried up to them. He was wearing a white button-down shirt and faded blue jeans with his trademark cowboy boots.

'I'm so glad I didn't miss you,' he said. 'Camilla had me running my lines with Garrick until late last night and I overslept.'

Olivia held up her purse. 'I've got my script here. She's a tough director, isn't she?'

'But good,' Jackson said. 'And I've worked with lots of directors.'

Ivy tried not to stare as Olivia and Jackson moved away to the lawn to talk privately for the last few minutes they had together this weekend.

Brendan grabbed her in a big bear hug from behind. 'See you later.'

'I'll call,' Ivy said.

Brendan waved and hopped on his bike.

Mr Vega took a step towards Olivia and

Jackson but Ivy stopped him. 'Just a couple more minutes.'

'OK,' he said. 'I'll programme the sat nav.'

Ivy tried to avoid watching the couple, but out of the corner of her eye, she saw Olivia rise up on her tiptoes. Ivy knew her sister hadn't had her first kiss yet and it looked like she was going for it right then and there!

In front of Dad! Ivy couldn't believe it.

Ivy glanced over to her dad, who seemed engrossed in his route-planning on the front seat, but he could look up at any moment.

Should she try to block his view or try to stop Olivia's kiss? Ivy looked back and forth between the lawn and the car; everything seemed in slow motion.

But then, she saw Jackson glancing sideways at the car. *He doesn't want to kiss her in front of Dad*, Ivy guessed.

Jackson did a last-minute ducking to the side, by-passing the kiss entirely and leaning all the way in for a hug.

Olivia looked like she'd just lost a winning lottery ticket.

'Have a great time,' Jackson said with a goofy wave and led Olivia back to the car. 'I'm jealous that you get to ride horses.'

Olivia brightened. 'I can't wait!'

'Bye,' Olivia called and turned to Ivy as Jackson's chauffeur opened the car door. 'Why oh why oh why won't he kiss me?' she whispered, as Jackson was driven off.

'What's that?' Mr Vega asked.

'Nothing!' Ivy called. 'Let's get on the road.' Ivy got in the front seat and Olivia sat in the back behind Mr Vega.

'Righty-oh,' Mr Vega called. 'Let's ride 'em, cowboy.'

The twins looked at each other and burst out laughing.

That just goes to show how vampires and country don't mix, Ivy thought. *But as long as it's not too bunny on the farm, this weekend should be fun.*

🦇　　🦇　　🦇

'Ooh, I love this song,' Olivia said, bopping around in the back seat to the twangy music blaring from the car speakers.

'It sounds like a dying hyena to me,' Ivy said, pretending to plug her ears.

'This is classic country music,' Mr Vega said. 'I made a playlist for the car journey, to get you in the mood.' He grinned, which on him looked a little sinister.

'Oh yes,' Ivy deadpanned. 'It makes my feet itch for some square dancing.'

'Ha ha,' Olivia replied. 'Itchy feet are no joking matter. The last time I had to deal with your itchy feet, you turned my Romeo from a Jackson Caulfield into a Garrick Stevens!'

'A prince to a frog,' Ivy quipped.

'Precisely,' Olivia said.

'Now, girls,' Mr Vega said, turning serious. 'You are, of course, able to come home at any time. If at any point you wish to leave, I can be there in half an hour.'

'Thanks, Dad,' Ivy said.

Olivia realised that Mr Vega was a little more worried about the weekend than his just-for-fun playlist suggested.

'You know that Aunt Rebecca doesn't know anything about . . . ah . . . our background,' he said.

'We know,' Olivia replied.

'She doesn't really understand why your mother and I didn't keep in touch with her. We were planning to tell her about you two once you were born. Things just didn't work out that way,' he finished sadly.

'Don't worry, Dad,' Ivy said. 'We get it. And we're really glad you tracked her down so we could meet her.'

Just then, a phone beeped.

'That's mine,' Mr Vega said. 'It's in my briefcase on the back seat. Olivia, will you answer it, please?'

Olivia fumbled for the phone and then pressed the green button. 'Charles Vega's phone,' she said.

'Ivy?' said a female voice. 'Olivia? It's Rebecca. Are you guys on your way? When will y'all get here?'

'It's Olivia and, uh . . . hang on.' She pressed the mute button. She didn't want Mr Vega to think that Rebecca was checking up on them, so she decided to rephrase the question. 'Aunt

Rebecca would like to know how far away we are.'

'We are on schedule, of course,' Mr Vega said, 'and will be arriving at 10 a.m. as discussed.'

'We're right on time,' Olivia translated, leaving out the 'of course' and 'as discussed' so that it didn't sound too defensive.

'Your dad's not expecting to stay for lunch, is he?' Rebecca wanted to know. 'We're going to be real busy as soon as you get here, and I wouldn't want him hanging around with nothing to do.'

Olivia pushed mute again. This was tricky to phrase. 'Rebecca says that lunch will probably be late so if you want to leave before then, she won't be offended.'

'That's kind of Rebecca,' Mr Vega replied. 'But I would like to have a look around Susannah's ranch. She told me so much about it.'

Drat, Olivia thought. If her bio-dad had been planning on just dropping them off, it would have made this conversation much easier.

'He'd like to see some of the ranch with us, if you don't mind,' Olivia told her aunt.

'Well, of course, that's fine,' Rebecca said but Olivia wondered if she didn't really want him to stay. 'I just wouldn't want him to get stuck in pre-lunch traffic on the way home.'

'Great,' Olivia chirped, deciding to end the conversation there. 'We'll see you soon.'

Ugh, Olivia thought. *That was awkward.*

Ivy offered a sympathetic look from the front seat.

It doesn't matter, Olivia thought to herself. *Finding out about our biological mom is going to be so worth it and we'll smooth out the adults' issues later.*

🦇　　　🦇　　　🦇

As Mr Vega stopped the car at the top of the ranch's driveway, Ivy's heart sank. There were animals everywhere.

Dozens of chickens ran free, pecking the ground, while two black Labradors lazed on the front porch. The stables were huge – it looked like a horse mansion. There were pigs in one pen and a goat was bleating as it munched on a green hedge.

This is definitely too much farm, Ivy thought to herself. *On the positive side, so far no cows to milk.*

As well as the animals, there were some picturesque weeping willow trees dotted around the yard. One overhung a small pond with a duck family swimming on it. It was like a scene from a painting.

Olivia looked like she'd just won a cheer-a-thon. Her eyes were sparkling as she undid her seatbelt and got out of the car. 'This is incredible!' Olivia declared.

'That's one word for it,' Ivy muttered as she followed, trying to avoid stepping on a white spotted chicken with feathers on either side of its head that looked like a beard.

It was a huge open space, and the wind was kicking up dust. The air smelled like weird popcorn and grass.

The two dogs snuffled and one let out a short bark. They bounded down from the porch swing to greet the visitors, but as they got nearer to Ivy, they backed off.

'Hello,' Olivia said softly to them. 'Who are you?'

That was all it took for the two big balls of fur to go straight to Olivia for a good scratching. Ivy knew that vampires sometimes had an effect on animals, but this seemed pretty extreme. The dogs didn't even want to come near her.

The screen door swung open and Rebecca rushed to greet them. She had flour on her hands and a breeze of apple-scent followed her.

'I just put dessert for tonight into the oven,' she said. 'Hope you like apple pie!'

'I love it,' declared Olivia as she gave Rebecca a hug.

One of the Labs growled as Ivy tried to step forwards for her hug.

'Gonzo! What's wrong with you?' Rebecca tugged on Gonzo's collar. 'Be nice to Ivy.'

Ivy smiled sheepishly. 'Dogs don't usually like me,' she admitted as Rebecca hugged her.

'Nonsense,' Rebecca replied. 'Gonzo likes everybody.'

That doesn't exactly make me feel better, Ivy thought, glad that the wind was whipping her hair in her face so that no one could tell she was disappointed.

'You didn't have to drive, Charlie,' Rebecca said. 'I would have been happy to pick them up.'

'It wasn't any trouble,' Mr Vega replied.

'Besides, I wanted to see this place that Susannah talked about so much.'

Ivy saw Rebecca wince at Susannah's name. *She must miss her every day*, Ivy thought. *I don't know how I could live without Olivia.*

'I just wish there was more of her presence here,' Rebecca said sadly. 'But we were here so long ago that it seems it's only my memories that keep her here.'

Mr Vega looked miserable, too. 'Sometimes the memories just aren't enough.'

Ivy didn't want this to turn into a funeral.

'Can we go and see the stables, now?' Olivia asked, clearly not wanting it to feel gloomy either.

It's not what I would have suggested, Ivy said, *but at least it will change the subject.*

'Of course,' Rebecca replied, perking up.

'I'll wait here and unload the luggage,' said Mr Vega. Ivy guessed he was feeling

91

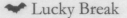

uncomfortable around the animals as well.

The four of them crunched across the dirt and gravel towards the huge wooden structure that seemed the size of a small supermarket.

It was cool and dark inside, with a long central walkway dividing a dozen individual stalls on either side. Two stable hands waved, one a man as old as their dad and the other was probably a high-school student. They were shovelling hay with pitchforks.

'That's Hank.' Rebecca pointed to the younger one. 'And that's John.'

There was a huge tackroom filled with saddles, buckets, blankets and other things.

'Wow,' Olivia breathed.

'We've got twenty-two horses in twenty-four stables,' Rebecca explained. 'It takes a lot of looking after.'

Ivy looked down the row at the horses. Every

single one of them was giant, magnificent and kind of scary. The nearest horse, tan with dark hair, shuffled and looked at Ivy warily. Ivy knew there were special terms for the descriptions of horses but she had no idea what they were.

'This is Coco,' Rebecca said of the tan one as they walked down the aisle. 'And this one is Admiral.' Admiral was all black with wise, cautious eyes.

Olivia greeted each one like a new best friend, and the horses whinnied and nuzzled back. Ivy kept her distance, not wanting a repeat of the scene with Gonzo.

'Come on, Ivy,' said Rebecca, walking over to a grey horse who had poked his nose over the stable door. 'Say hi to Leo. He's as gentle as a lamb.'

Ivy forced a smile. *A lamb three times the size of me with stompy feet*, she thought.

Rebecca opened Leo's stall, took hold of his

harness and led him out into the wide aisle. The horse tossed his dark grey mane and snorted. His hooves clomped on the floor and he kept watching Ivy.

She gulped.

'Don't worry,' Rebecca said. 'Give him a pet.'

If Olivia can do this, Ivy thought, *and if my mother could do this, then so can I.* She shuffled forwards, and held out her hand but it was shaking.

The horse side-stepped away from her, and Ivy's heart sank.

Rebecca clicked her tongue and Olivia was smiling encouragingly. Ivy took a deep breath and the horse seemed to calm down a little.

Ivy reached out again and this time, she touched the side of the horse's neck. The short hair was almost wiry and Ivy could feel the strength in the animal's muscles.

Wow, she thought. *That's amazing.* Ivy had

always thought horses were beautiful, but she'd never been close enough to touch one.

Bang!

The door to the barn slammed open in the wind, which startled several of the horses, including Leo. He reared up, kicking his front feet and jerking his head. Rebecca lost her grip on his harness and he bolted out of the open door.

Ivy leaped back, falling against a wooden pillar, and Olivia dived out of the way into a pile of hay.

The two stable hands jumped to attention, rushing out into the yard to try to catch the frightened horse.

'Oh my goodness, girls!' Rebecca rushed over to Ivy. 'Are you OK?'

Ivy nodded and looked for Olivia.

Olivia brushed herself down. 'I'm fine,' she confirmed.

'Leo is never usually jumpy,' Rebecca said, helping Ivy up.

I know exactly what's making him jumpy now, Ivy thought. Rebecca had no idea that Ivy was a vampire, but the horse could obviously sense it.

As they rushed towards the open stable door to see what had happened to the horse, Ivy wanted to keep on running, just like Leo.

I'm a walking farm disaster! Ivy thought.

Chapter Five

Standing in the stable doorway, the bright sunshine blinded Ivy momentarily.

She heard a sharp whistle and a horse whinnying. Then her eyes adjusted – and nearly fell out of her head.

She saw her father holding on to Leo's harness, stroking his neck and talking to him softly. Leo seemed perfectly at ease now, not at all afraid of her dad.

Great, Ivy thought. *It's not vampires; it's just me. And how does Dad know how to stop a runaway horse?*

Mr Vega led Leo back towards the barn.

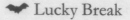

'I didn't know you handled horses,' Rebecca said to him.

'Susannah loved to ride,' he said simply.

Ivy guessed that it was also because he was born close to two hundred years ago, when everyone rode horses instead of motorbikes.

'What happened in there?' Mr Vega wanted to know.

'I –' Ivy began but Rebecca leaped in. 'I don't know. Leo just bolted,' she said.

Mr Vega looked concerned. 'You know my girls are not experienced horsewomen.'

'Of course,' Rebecca spluttered. 'I would never do anything to endanger them.'

Mr Vega passed Leo over to the older stable hand.

Ivy felt even worse. The adults didn't need anything to add to their pile of disagreements.

'I'll leave you to it and head home now,' he

said to Ivy and Olivia. 'Are you sure you're going to be OK?'

No! No, I'm not! Just take me home. That's what Ivy wanted to say, but there was no way she could drag Olivia away from the farm when she was so clearly loving everything about it. Plus, Rebecca was her mom's twin. She would force herself to stick it out for the one night.

He hugged them both goodbye and nodded to Rebecca. 'I'll pick them up tomorrow at six. Keep them safe.'

'You don't have anything to worry about,' Rebecca said, smiling tightly. Ivy could see how tense her aunt's body was.

They waved as Mr Vega drove away in a cloud of dust.

Ivy kept watching until the car was a dot on the horizon. Then she turned back to the chaos of chickens, goats, dogs and horses. One fat brown hen pecked its way over to her, and Ivy swore it was clucking its disapproval.

'Are you OK to look at the rest of the horses?' Rebecca said. 'There's one in particular I want you to meet.'

Olivia put her hand on Ivy's arm, to ask the question silently.

Ivy wasn't sure. She didn't want to scare them or humiliate herself again.

'Your mom's favourite horse is the old patriarch of the stable now. I've started to think he was sticking around to meet you both.'

Ivy's eyes met Olivia's. Their mother's favourite horse!

'Your mom helped birth Lucky,' Rebecca explained, wrestling playfully with the two energetic Labs. 'It was a close call, too. Lucky's legs were in the wrong position and he was in danger of not making it. Your mom wouldn't give up, though, and he survived.'

Ivy was a little afraid to do it, but she had to meet the horse that meant so much to her mother. 'Yes, I want to meet Lucky,' she blurted.

'Me too,' Olivia whispered.

They walked through the stable to the back. Lucky was munching on some feed in the last stall. He was beautiful — all white, including his mane. His big black eyes, full of grace and dignity, seemed to take everything in.

'He was a jumping champion in his youth,' Rebecca said, pointing to several framed photos outside his stall.

Ivy caught her breath. In each picture, their mom was standing next to Lucky, as a girl not much older than Ivy was now. She was always holding up trophies or flower bouquets, except for one photo where it was simply Susannah hugging Lucky.

The horse snorted gently as Rebecca spoke to him and stroked his muzzle. 'Hello, lovely Lucky,' she said. 'Look who I've brought you.' Lucky nudged Rebecca with her nose. 'This is Olivia and Ivy – Susannah's girls.'

'Hi, Lucky,' Olivia said.

'Hello,' Ivy whispered, not wanting to ruin the moment. Lucky swung his head over to them and blinked.

Not exactly an excited welcome, Ivy thought, *but at least he isn't trying to run away.*

'He would always jump higher and ride better for your mom. It was like Lucky thought Susannah was *his* mom.'

Olivia gasped. 'That practically makes him our brother!'

Lucky snorted, and Ivy couldn't tell if that meant he was agreeing or thought it was a ridiculous idea.

'I don't ride Lucky too much nowadays. He's very old and a bit frail. He needs a dose of medicine every day, and loves his creature comforts!' Rebecca said. 'But how about if we take out a couple of the younger horses for a little trot?'

'Yes, please!' Olivia said.

'I'll just watch for now,' Ivy replied. 'One horse not attempting to flee is a victory for me. I don't want to push my luck.'

'Ha ha,' said Olivia at the pun.

Ivy sat on a bench, swinging her feet, as Olivia and Rebecca 'tacked up' their two horses. Bits, pommels and cruppers – it all sounded like Romanian to her, but Olivia seemed to be picking it up easily.

While Rebecca led Coco and Olivia took Honey, a light-golden horse, into the yard for a ride, Ivy perched on the fence and watched as they laughed and chatted. The wind rustled through the woods behind them and picked up little flurries of dust wherever the horses stepped. Ivy was a long way from her bedroom coffin.

'Looking at you riding, here on the ranch . . .' Rebecca called to Olivia. 'You remind me so much of your mother. It's like I'm looking at a thirteen-year-old version of Susannah.'

Olivia beamed and Ivy couldn't help it; she felt a pang of jealousy. *Don't I remind her of our mother, too?*

'Ivy, watch!' Olivia called and urged Honey into a canter.

Ivy gave a little wave. Olivia was a natural and looked like she was having the time of her life. Normally Ivy would be happy sitting on the sidelines – especially at something as bunny-ish as a farm – but this was her mom's favourite place.

I want at least some part of this to make sense to me. Ivy looked at the pigs rolling around in the mud, snorting gleefully. The leaves of the big weeping willow tree were so long that they made a tent around the trunk. Ivy wandered over to sit underneath the tree. She could still see the riders but it was through a curtain of green.

The main riff from *Phantom of the Opera* intoned from her messenger bag and she pulled out her phone. She already knew it was Brendan.

'How ya doin', cowgirl?' Brendan said in a fake drawl.

She sighed. Rebecca and Olivia were lost in their own equine world and couldn't hear her conversation, so she could be honest. 'Like a cow without its spots, or a chicken without its feathers – utterly out of place.'

'Uh-oh,' Brendan said. 'That doesn't sound good.'

Ivy turned away from the riders, holding back tears. 'I should have known I wouldn't fit in, but this kind of bites.' She took a breath.

'I'm coming,' Brendan declared, his voice serious now. 'Where are you?'

'You can't; I'm miles away.' Ivy sniffled.

'There is this incredible invention called the wheel – and I am the proud owner of two.'

Ivy smiled. Brendan could always cheer her up.

'In fact, these two wheels have a chain and pedals that take me wherever I want to go. Now,' he instructed, 'tell me where you are.'

Ivy glanced back to see Rebecca and Olivia riding side by side. 'I could do with the company.' She told him the address.

'See you as soon as I can,' Brendan said and hung up.

Olivia wiped the tears from her eyes and kept chopping. She had a stack of onions to get through for the tomato and bean soup that Aunt Rebecca was making for dinner.

Ivy was dicing up the tomatoes from Rebecca's garden like a professional chef and, for the first time since they'd arrived, Olivia saw her sister had relaxed. Ever since Gonzo growled at her, Ivy had been walking around afraid to touch anything in case she broke it.

But now the three of them were sitting on tall stools around the island in the middle of the huge country kitchen. There was a basket of fresh eggs on the windowsill, rustic wooden cabinets and a huge open stove. They were surrounded by fresh ingredients for the soup: chives, potatoes and carrots, all from Rebecca's garden.

'Ivy, you are a whiz with that knife,' Rebecca commented as she washed and drained the beans in front of the kitchen window.

'I like cooking,' Ivy replied. 'And this knife makes it easy. It's a Fangtooth knife, right?'

Olivia wondered if that was a vampire-run company. There were all sorts of them, from the Milk Duds baby store to funeral homes that were more like bedroom displays – seemingly normal, but with a vampire store in the basement.

'It sure is. Your mom always used to say that you had to have the right tools for the job,' Rebecca replied, and Olivia felt a little lurch.

Every time Rebecca said something like that, it was like another piece of the puzzle fell into place, like her mother was that much more real.

'Will you tell us another story about her?' Olivia asked. 'About when you both came here?'

Rebecca put down the beans. 'I can tell you that she always used to tease me for being a vegetarian and she was a terrible cook. She tried to make chocolate-chip cookies once and used baking soda instead of flour. Ugh!'

Olivia chuckled. 'That must have tasted horrible.'

'The funniest part was she was so determined to prove that she could cook, she ate a whole cookie, pretending it tasted wonderful.' Rebecca smiled.

'From the looks of that apple pie,' Olivia replied, 'you obviously know what you're doing in the kitchen.'

'Thanks,' Rebecca said. 'But that's enough about me. I want to know everything about you.' She started to put ingredients into a big blue pot on the stove. 'Ivy, will you go first?'

'I don't know what to tell,' she said.

'Then, I'll do it for you,' Olivia said, carrying over her onions. 'Ivy is the best writer on the school newspaper. She's in all advanced classes and has read lots of the classic literature books I wish I had, like Jane Austen.'

Rebecca beamed at Ivy. 'Your mother read Jane Austen.'

'Really?' Ivy said, like she'd just won the lottery.

Olivia was glad to see her perking up – well, as much as a broody vampire could perk.

'She read all that stuff,' Rebecca said. 'I could never understand it.'

Olivia watched her sister turn back to her tomato-chopping with twice the enthusiasm, while Rebecca stirred the soup with her big wooden spoon.

'I always wondered . . .' but Rebecca's voice trailed off as she peered out of the window. 'Is that . . .? Who could that be?' She pointed with the spoon and a piece of cooked carrot plopped on to the counter.

'Who?' Olivia couldn't see.

'There's some hooligan in black stalking my chickens!' Rebecca cried.

Ivy ran to look out of the window. 'He's here!' She jumped up and down, her boots clomping on the blue-and-white tile floor, then rushed for the door.

'Oh dear,' Rebecca said, frowning, as they followed her out of the kitchen. 'That's Ivy's boyfriend, isn't it?'

'Don't worry,' Olivia said. 'Ivy's too excited to take any offence at the hooligan comment.'

'It's all that black he wears,' Rebecca muttered as she hurried down the hallway.

Olivia cleared her throat. 'It's not what you wear that makes you a thug.'

When Olivia and Rebecca got to the front door, Ivy had jumped into Brendan's arms to give him a huge hug and he was twirling her around.

He put her down when he noticed Rebecca

and said, 'I hope you don't mind, Ms Kendall, and I won't stay long. I've left my bike by your mailbox.'

He didn't look at all tired from his bike ride, but that was one of the advantages of vampire super-strength.

Rebecca cleared her throat. 'No, no, I don't mind.'

Olivia wondered if she was telling the truth. But Olivia knew that after Aunt Rebecca had spent some time with Brendan, she'd see past his clothes to know how nice he was.

'Thanks, Aunt Rebecca,' Ivy said. 'Brendan really . . . uh . . . really loves horses.'

Brendan whipped his head up in surprise, but covered it up quickly. 'Drawing them,' he said. 'Not riding them.'

'OK, then,' Rebecca replied, unconvinced. 'I'll just go add more beans to the soup.' She gave an awkward smile and went back into the house.

'So, what's really going on?' Olivia said to Ivy and Brendan.

'I was feeling like a third wheel,' Ivy confessed. 'A fifth wheel, really: you, Rebecca, Coco and Honey were having so much fun.'

'I could tell she wasn't,' Brendan put in, 'so I insisted on coming. Besides, I wanted to see my girl living the cowgirl life!'

'I'm sorry this hasn't been easy for you,' Olivia said. She felt awful that her sister wasn't enjoying herself. She didn't want it to be like when they went to meet their vampire family in Transylvania and Ivy had felt like an outsider.

'It's fine,' Ivy replied. 'I never expected to do the horse thing. At least my mom and I have Jane Austen in common.'

As they headed back into the house, Olivia saw Brendan grab hold of Ivy's hand.

I wish I'd thought of inviting Jackson, Olivia thought, and decided to send him a text message. She took her phone out of her pocket but there was already a message from him waiting for her: *Headline: Franklin Grove 27 per cent less cool without Olivia Abbott. Entire town awaits her return.*

She smiled and replied: *The horses are so beautiful. You have to come out here at some point. Miss you tons.* She paused then finished: *XXX.*

Maybe, she thought, *I should be even more obvious and write out: Kiss, kiss, kiss. And don't make my first kiss be with Garrick!*

'Come inside,' Rebecca called. 'And help me finish up the soup.'

They trooped down the hall into the kitchen; the smell of onions had started to fill the air. Brendan had to duck to avoid the copper pots that were hanging from the ceiling, and definitely looked out of place next to the blue-

and-red checked tablecloth.

'What can I do?' Brendan offered.

'Nothing, nothing,' Rebecca insisted, so Brendan sat down at the table awkwardly.

'So, Ivy . . . Olivia gave me the summary all about you,' Rebecca said, snipping up chives into the soup pot. 'Why don't you give me the rundown on your sister?'

Ivy pretended to think hard. 'Well, she's a neat freak, much too cheerful in the morning and has a flare for extravagant party planning.'

Olivia smiled. Ivy was such a cute grump.

'Oh yeah, and — as you know — she's dating the most famous movie star in the whole world.'

Rebecca clapped. 'I know!' she squealed and turned to Olivia. 'Tell me all about it.'

That wasn't something Olivia had trouble talking about at all. She launched into the story

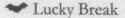

of how they'd met, when he'd dressed up as a security guard.

But a nagging voice at the back of her mind kept piping up: *He still hasn't kissed you yet!*

Ivy and Brendan sat quietly while Olivia and Rebecca babbled on about cheerleading, horses and Jackson. Gonzo and Gibson, the Labradors, kept an eye on them from matching baskets in the corner of the kitchen.

'So, Brendan,' Rebecca said in a rare lull in the bunny conversation. 'Why don't you tell me a little about you?'

Brendan pushed his curly hair away from his face. 'Well, uh, there's not much to tell. I like running and am kind of a science geek, like my dad – chemistry, building stuff.'

'Are you in any after-school clubs?' Rebecca asked.

Brendan shook his head. 'The kind of stuff I like tends to be less crowded.'

'He plays a mean game of air hockey,' Ivy put in.

Rebecca didn't look impressed.

It's not fair, Ivy thought to herself. Comparing Brendan to Jackson was like comparing funeral wreaths to wedding bouquets. *Jackson might be the most amazing guy according to the entire world, but Brendan takes me by surprise every day.*

'Aunt Rebecca,' Ivy said. 'Do you mind if I take Brendan on a little walk around the yard before he rides home? We promise not to disturb any of the animals.'

At least, she hoped they wouldn't.

'Of course, sweetie.' Rebecca looked relieved, either that they were going for a walk or that he was going to ride home. *Probably both*, Ivy thought. 'It makes sense to head out long before sunset.'

Ivy remembered Rebecca saying something similar to her dad.

'Do you want to come, Olivia?' Ivy asked.

Olivia shook her head and held up her script. 'I was going to run through my Juliet lines.'

'Ooh, can I help?' Rebecca offered.

'Sure!' Olivia replied and handed over the papers.

Brendan grabbed Ivy's lightweight buckled coat, and they headed out on to the front porch.

The sun was low and the sky was turning yellow.

'I think your aunt doesn't like me much,' Brendan said, as they wandered past one of the weeping willow trees casting shadows across the yard.

'She thought you were stalking her chickens.'

Brendan chuckled. 'They are some crazy-looking chickens.'

'She doesn't seem to be a big fan of black,' Ivy said. 'She doesn't like my dad much either. But she is really nice, and she's already told us a ton about our mom that we never knew. Olivia is loving every minute.'

Brendan nodded. 'There might be parts of your mom that Olivia understands better, but there are parts just for you, too.'

Ivy thought of Jane Austen again. 'You're right.'

'And you're beautiful,' Brendan replied, giving her a little kiss on the nose. 'I'd better go, before the sun sets and either my bike turns into a pumpkin, or I turn into a chicken-stalking zombie . . . Grr arrg!' He held up his hands and pretended to chase Ivy.

She dashed under the willow tree branches, back up the steps and collapsed giggling on to the porch swing.

Brendan kissed her and then headed off

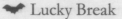

into the sunset, like a cowboy. Well, a black-clad vampire cowboy on a bike.

'Thanks for coming,' she called after him. He did a wheelie in reply, sending up a cloud of dust.

She snuggled into the cushions and gently swung back and forth, watching the sun go down. She could see why her mother would have loved coming here. The ranch was beautiful.

Ivy wished she had her notebook, but it was upstairs in her backpack. She felt like this swing would be the perfect place to write.

She sat for another moment, enjoying the changing colours of the sky. Then Olivia and Rebecca burst out laughing inside. Ivy hopped down from the swing to join them. She took a step. Her foot hit a floorboard that was poking up and she ended up sprawled across the porch. Ivy twisted round to look back over her shoulder; she'd dislodged the wooden plank.

Great, Ivy thought. *Now I'm destroying the house!*

Ivy crouched down and saw that there were no nails at either end of the board. It had been loose for a while. When she went to slot it back in place, she realised why. There was something hidden under the plank. She took out her cell phone and used the light of its screen to see a battered journal wrapped in a clear plastic bag. As she pulled it out, she could see that its leather cover was embossed with the initials 'S.K.'

Susannah Kendall.

Ivy sucked in her breath.

She'd just found a journal that belonged to her and Olivia's biological mom!

Chapter Six

The instant Aunt Rebecca shut the door to their top-floor bedroom, Ivy leaped off the red-and-white quilt of the bed they were supposed to share.

'I have been desperate to tell you this for the last *eternity*!' she declared.

Olivia was completely taken by surprise and almost backed into the white drawers covered in odd knick-knacks, like rainbow-coloured ceramic cows and a statue of an African drummer.

Ivy never got this excited unless it was something big.

'What is it?' Olivia asked.

'This.' Ivy held up a dirty plastic bag that smelled like mud.

'Uh . . .' Olivia had no idea what it could be.

'Look!' Ivy thrust it closer to her face and Olivia actually did bump into the drawers.

But then she saw what had Ivy hopping about like a cricket.

There were initials on the cover of the book inside the bag. 'S.K.'

'Is that what I think it is?' Olivia whispered.

'I think so,' Ivy whispered back. 'It was hidden in the porch and it looks old.'

'More than thirteen years old,' Olivia agreed.

'I waited for you to look at it, but . . .' Ivy hesitated. 'I didn't want to show it to Aunt Rebecca just yet. I think this might be too big to share before we really know what it is.'

Olivia nodded. Her heart was racing like she'd

just landed a back flip. 'We can show it to her tomorrow.'

'Can we . . .?' Ivy said at the same time as Olivia started, 'Should we . . .?'

They both wanted to read it. They *had* to read it . . . to see if it really was their mom's.

'You do it,' Olivia offered. 'You're the one who found it.'

Ivy gingerly peeled the plastic back and pulled out the notebook. Around the initials, there was a faded pattern of ivy embossed on the brown leather.

'Ivy,' Olivia whispered.

Ivy carried the journal ceremoniously over to the bed. Olivia sat down on the quilt beside her and Ivy opened the first page. It was filled with line after line of scribbly, narrow lettering:

First day at the ranch. Twenty-two days until I'm fourteen.

Ivy and Olivia looked at each other. The last time they found a journal from their family past, it revealed the secret of who their real parents were. Olivia knew she wouldn't find out anything as dramatic, but it would be a precious glimpse of their mom.

This is so awesome! Mom gave me this new journal when we arrived. I've decided to keep this just for the farm and go back to my comp books when we go home. I've never had a leather journal before. It's gooorgeous!

Rebecca got a new set of paints. She said she wasn't going to have time for painting – I bet she won't. She's already in the stables.

'This is the best thing ever,' Olivia declared.

Ivy's eyes shone. 'I am going to read this cover to cover – but maybe not all at once.'

'We should do it together,' Olivia said and Ivy nodded.

'Let's go through the rest of this entry,' Ivy said.

We're here for six weeks, but I've only brought four books. I'll make Mom take me to the library. We're going to have lunch soon, I think. Burgers on the BBQ and corn on the cob – yum!

Corn on the cob wasn't exactly deep motherly wisdom, but Olivia felt like her mom was right there speaking – and that was practically a miracle.

The next morning, during their breakfast of just-laid farm eggs and freshly baked bread, Ivy produced the journal. The girls had decided before they went to sleep that they would tell Aunt Rebecca about it.

'Oh my goodness,' Rebecca said, reaching out to touch the soft cover. 'Is this . . .?'

Olivia and Ivy nodded at the same time.

'Where did you find it?' she breathed, pushing aside her half-eaten omelette.

'Under a floorboard by the porch swing,' Ivy said, her scrambled eggs forgotten.

'Susannah was always writing in journals in that swing.' Rebecca's hand lingered over the cover but then pulled away. 'I am so tempted to read it, but I never knew what she wrote in there – and no one wants their sister reading her journal.' She sat back in her chair. 'But you two should; daughters are definitely allowed.'

Ivy and Olivia shared a guilty look.

'And if there's anything you want to ask me about, I'll try to help as much as I can.'

'Thanks,' Ivy said. 'We want to know as much about our mom as there is to know.' Finally Ivy felt like there was a reason she was supposed to have come here.

Rebecca cleared her throat. 'Girls, I hope you don't think it's too much – and I hope your parents will agree – but I'd really like you to come back again.'

'Me too,' Olivia said, without hesitation.

'If we left the journal here,' Ivy said slowly, 'we could come back again next weekend to read it.'

'That would be perfect,' Rebecca said, smiling. 'And to make the journey worth your while, Ivy, I'm going to get you up on a horse.'

'I don't know about that,' Ivy replied, turning her attention back to the food. She broke open a freshly baked roll and steam rose up from the soft middle.

'Trust me,' Rebecca said with a smile. 'There's never been a person that I couldn't match with a horse.'

Ivy forced a smile. *Yeah, but how many vampires do you know?*

Ivy was just throwing her toothbrush in her bag when Aunt Rebecca flew in the door. 'Your dad is coming up the driveway!'

'Whoops!' Ivy said. 'I'm not ready yet.'

Olivia and Rebecca had spent the morning with the horses and after that, once they'd started reading their mom's journal, Ivy had lost track of time.

The entries they read were about taking care of the chickens and the goats, a crush that she'd had on an older guy at school and how one of the horses – which would turn out to be Lucky's mom – was pregnant.

Ivy tossed in a pair of socks that was lying on the floor, zipped up her bag and followed Rebecca down the steps with Olivia just behind.

They managed to make it to the porch by the time Mr Vega stepped out of the car, against the backdrop of the sunset.

'Didn't you say seven?' Rebecca asked, brushing her hair out of her face.

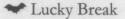

'I definitely said six,' Mr Vega replied.

'I could have sworn you said seven.' Rebecca picked up Olivia's bag and took it over to the car.

Mr Vega cleared his throat and then went over to get Ivy's bag. Once the luggage was stowed in the boot, he said, 'I'm sure you'll see the girls again soon.'

Rebecca was about to reply. Ivy jumped in, 'We were kind of hoping that we could come back next weekend.'

She realised that she actually meant it. She wanted to read that journal and did want to see if Rebecca could help her with the horses. *I must have liked it here, after all*, she thought. *At least a little bit.*

Mr Vega frowned. 'Oh. Well, ah. I suppose so.'

'I'll let you know what my parents say,' Olivia called as she got into the car.

As Ivy climbed in, she almost sat on a

brown paper bag. 'What's this?'

'Oh, just a little something,' said Mr Vega.

Ivy waved goodbye to Rebecca and the farm and turned to her package. It was a new concert album from Mountain of Beef, one of her favourite bands.

'Wow, thanks!' Olivia called from the backseat.

Her sister was holding a book called *Method Acting for Beginners*.

'Just a little something,' Mr Vegas said, his face colouring as he kept his eyes on the road.

The twins shared a look. They didn't normally receive presents for no reason.

Is Dad feeling threatened? Ivy wondered. She made a mental note to make sure she did a father/daughter dinner this week, in between play rehearsals. She knew what it was like to feel left out. *I don't want Dad to feel like that at all.*

🦇　　　🦇　　　🦇

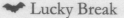

'Tighter,' commanded Camilla.

Sophia, who was fitting Olivia's robot costume, squeezed the golden corset-type top even more. Olivia thought she was never going to breathe again.

'Too tight! A little too tight!' she gasped. She loved her Julietron outfit – especially the gold, knee-high boots – but this was crazy!

Sophia relaxed it a little and Camilla frowned. 'I suppose I need you to be able to say your lines,' she said.

Thank goodness for that, Olivia thought.

'It looks great,' Camilla told Sophia. She was wearing black tuxedo bottoms and a white button-down shirt, with her now trademark red braces. 'And you were born to play my Juliet, Olivia.'

'Thanks!' said Sophia and Olivia at the same time.

On the other side of the small dressing room,

Charlotte snorted.

'Born to kiss Garrick Stevens,' she muttered.

Charlotte hadn't missed an opportunity to rub that in ever since the roles had been announced a week and a half ago.

'I need at least one more layer of padding in Charlotte's costume,' Camilla declared.

Olivia stifled a smile. Charlotte's balloon-like Nanny-bot costume had gone from the size of a normal television to a wide-screen deluxe during this final costume fitting.

'I'm not going to be able to move!' Charlotte wailed. The costume engulfed her up to her elbows and knees, so she had to waddle.

'Trust me,' Camilla said. 'You're going to look like the perfect old lady robot.'

'Great,' Charlotte said. 'Just the look I was going for.'

'I'm going to check on the boys,' Camilla

said. 'You're doing a fabulous job, Sophia.' Sophia beamed. 'You two,' Camilla said to Olivia and Charlotte, 'have about five minutes to get changed and get out into the studio for our final blocking rehearsal.'

They had been pacing out each scene in the last few rehearsals and Camilla had told them she wanted to finalise it today so they could start full run-throughs tomorrow.

Sophia started to help Charlotte get out of her puff-ball costume.

'Would you say Juliet is more like a gazelle or a swan?' asked Olivia, placing her boots neatly on the shelf.

'I would say your Juliet is more like a golden goose,' Sophia replied, picking up the Nanny-bot wig where Charlotte had tossed it. 'Why do you ask?'

'It's just that this method acting book my bio-dad got for me,' Olivia explained, 'says that actors can model their movements on animals.'

'If that's the case,' Sophia whispered, 'then Charlotte should be thinking hippo.'

🦇   🦇   🦇

Four minutes later, when Olivia walked into the studio, Jackson and Garrick were rehearsing an early scene. It was the one just before Romezog met Julietron at the masked ball.

'Nay, gentle Romezog, we must have you dance,' said Jackson, pretending to play with the many arms that Garrick's costume – once he was wearing it – would have.

'Not I, believe me,' read Garrick from a scruffy-looking script, standing stock-still. 'You have . . . uh . . . dancing shoes with nimble soles; I have a soul of lead, so stakes me . . .' He paused to look up and chuckle. 'Stakes . . .' he repeated. When no one else seemed to think the joke was

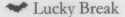

funny, he carried on. 'Uh . . . stakes me to the ground I cannot move.'

Camilla looked like she was about to strangle him. 'Garrick, you are staying for extra rehearsals this afternoon,' she ordered.

'But my band is supposed to jam tonight,' he whined.

'Until you are off script,' Camilla said, 'and can do the entire play from memory, you will be stuck here with me *every* afternoon. Now, continue!'

As they went on, Olivia's stomach churned like a Mister Smoothie mixer.

Garrick was the least romantic Romeo in all of history. He might make a great twitchy alien, but there was nothing appealing about his spotty skin or his lecherous grins. At least she'd been able to avoid kissing him so far.

Jackson, on the other hand, looked amazing, delivering his lines with confidence. He still hadn't tried to kiss her and Olivia was starting to worry that she wouldn't be able to avoid Garrick for much longer.

'I dream'd a dream tonight,' read Garrick.

'And so did I,' replied Jackson.

'Well, what was yours?' Garrick sounded more like a petulant child than a Shakespearean actor.

'That dreamers often lie.' Jackson put his hands together and tucked them under his ear, like he was sleeping on a pillow, but emphasising the double meaning of 'lic'.

It's so unfair! Olivia thought. *Jackson can get across two meanings while Garrick can't even get across one. Think how good a Romeo Jackson would have made!*

It wasn't long before Olivia took the stage across from Garrick for the Romezog and Julietron scene where they meet at the ball and fall in love at first sight. There were boxes set up to represent the tables and the neon light fountain that would be on stage for the real thing.

Camilla and some of the other cast members were sitting in plastic seats to watch.

'Are you ready?' asked Camilla.

'Uh, huh, huh . . .' Garrick chuckled his helicopter laugh again. 'Just a sec.'

He reached into his pocket, pulled out a familiar-looking bag and tipped a little powder down his trousers. Immediately, he started hopping around like a flea. He was using the itching powder to stay in character, taking method acting to a whole new level.

'Let's start from Tybalt's exit!' Camilla commanded.

They began rehearsing Romeo and Juliet's first meeting.

'O, then, dear saint, let lips do what hands do!' Garrick twitched nearer and nearer with every word. 'They pray; grant thou, lest faith turn to despair,' he said in a monotone.

Unlike the previous scenes, Garrick had all these lines memorised. *Probably*, Olivia thought, *because he read the kissing parts over and over again. Ew.* But he was just saying them, without any feeling. Olivia wondered if Garrick even knew what he was saying.

Olivia had to hold on to all her willpower to stay in character and not cringe as she said her line, 'Saints do not move, though grant for prayers' sake.'

'Then move not, while my prayer's effect I take.' Garrick leered at her.

Olivia felt her mouth go dry. That was the line just before Romeo kisses Juliet.

'Thus from my lips, by thine, my sin is purg'd.' Garrick leaned in and Olivia turned it into a quick air-kiss – even that made her want to projectile vomit.

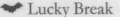

'Cut, cut!' Camilla cried, waving her hands. 'Olivia, you are way too human. You're supposed to be a robot! And why aren't you two actually kissing? There's only a week until final dress rehearsal. I need to see the real love, the real passion.'

Olivia almost gagged – love, passion? With Garrick?

'Run those lines again,' Camilla directed.

It looked like Olivia was about one minute away from having her first kiss – with the wrong guy.

'But . . . but . . .' Olivia stammered.

Do something! she thought. It was too late to pretend to be ill; the fire alarm was in the other room; Camilla would kill her if she disrupted rehearsals.

'I'm having trouble with my motivation,' Olivia blurted. 'Would a robot really kiss an alien? Robots don't have feelings.'

Camilla practically shrieked, 'That's what makes it romantic! It's the whole point!'

Olivia looked around for support, but Jackson must have gone for a costume fitting. Ivy was somewhere painting the set and Charlotte was giggling in the corner.

Ugh.

'I completely agree, Ms Edmunson,' Garrick said, still wiggling around from the itching powder. 'It's very romantic.' He opened his arms to Olivia. 'Now, come here and give me a big kiss.'

Olivia felt a little bile rise up from her stomach. Kissing a boy who would actually put itching powder down his own jeans! Gross.

'We can't just kiss,' Olivia protested, stalling for time. 'You have to say the lines.'

'Fine: thus from my lips, by thine, my sin is purg'd. Now, c'mere.' He hopped a jerky dance towards her. His breath smelled like bacon.

Three . . . two . . . one . . .

At last, an idea came!

Olivia shrieked at the top of her lungs. Garrick recoiled and Camilla jumped out of her seat. Olivia felt a tiny bit guilty, but she'd started now and couldn't stop.

'Itch! Itching everywhere!' Olivia shouted, pretending to scratch herself. 'It must have been his powder!'

'Oh no!' Camilla said. 'Get to the bathroom!'

Olivia didn't need telling twice. She bolted from the studio and rushed to the nearest girls' bathroom. It took her a moment to catch her breath, so she leaned against the sink and was still standing there when Camilla opened the door.

Olivia tried to grab paper towels, but it was too late.

'You weren't really itching, were you?' Camilla asked softly.

Olivia bit her lip and shook her head.

Camilla sighed. 'I'm sorry; I do get really bossy when I'm in director mode.'

'It's not a bad thing,' Olivia replied. 'Jackson thinks you're as good as a Hollywood director.'

Camilla blushed, then hopped up on the sink counter. 'What's really going on?'

'I totally get why you picked Garrick, but I just *can't* kiss him a hundred times a day.' The very thought brought the bile back. 'It's the most foul thing ever.'

Camilla thought for a moment. 'No problem,' she declared and Olivia wanted to weep with relief. 'I can write out most of the kisses – and you don't have to do it for real in rehearsal.'

Olivia almost broke into a cheer, until Camilla said, 'But there's no way of taking out the last kiss, in the last scene. You will have to kiss Garrick once for the performance.'

Olivia sighed.

'Is there something you're not telling me?' Camilla prompted. 'I may be your director, but I'm your friend first.'

Olivia confessed about not having kissed Jackson yet. 'Having Garrick Stevens as my first kiss would be worth disconnecting my power supply to prevent.'

'Hm,' Camilla said. 'That does present a problem. But it's nothing a little cyborg stalking can't fix.'

'Huh?'

'You've got about ten days before the performance, right?' Camilla prompted.

'Right,' Olivia agreed.

'That means you have approximately two hundred and forty hours to get your dream hunk cyborg boyfriend to kiss you,' she explained. 'Preferably more than once. That way, Garrick's kiss will be a blip on the radar screen of love.'

Olivia giggled. 'Only you could explain it like that.'

Camilla winked at her. 'I have to get back,' she said, jumping down. 'See you in a few minutes?'

Olivia nodded and Camilla left.

She looked at herself in the mirror. *Two hundred and forty hours*. Camilla was right. Her new mission was to get Jackson to kiss her – at all costs.

Chapter Seven

'Where is he?' Olivia said aloud, searching through the crowds of students leaving their after-school activities. She was on the top step, just outside the huge school doors, but couldn't spot her boyfriend anywhere.

She'd successfully fended off Garrick for the remainder of the rehearsal and Camilla praised her when she tried out the gazelle plus robot movements.

But when Camilla had let them go, Jackson had darted off, thwarting her efforts to put Operation Cyborg Smooching into action.

'There!'

He was wearing a crash helmet with a visor to avoid being recognised by any eager fans, but she knew his light-blue eco-warrior shirt. He was unlocking his bike from the rack.

She bolted down the steps, narrowly missing knocking over a sixth-grader carrying some science experiment involving lots of glass tubes and something that smelled like rotten eggs.

'Hey!' she called to Jackson.

'Olivia!' He pushed up the visor and grinned. 'I thought you'd already left.'

Kiss me, kiss me! She wanted to shout, but she had to stay casual. 'Nope, still here.'

'Well, see you tomorrow,' he said, giving her a hug.

'How about not?' she said. 'I mean, how about seeing me now?'

Jackson looked confused. 'Do you mean in

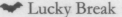

some other way than me looking at you looking at me?'

Arg! Why is this so complicated? Olivia thought. 'Yes, I mean, do you want to go to the mall? For a snack or something? Do you have time?'

'Time for my beautiful girlfriend?' he said. 'Of course.'

They sat down in the food court at a corner table, with Jackson facing the wall to minimise how often he got recognised.

Olivia was chewing on her fingernails again.

She'd tried to kiss him on the walk over, but with him wheeling his bike, it was hard to get into range. When they'd walked past the fountain in the mall, she thought he was going to kiss her, but he was just looking at the tennis rackets in the window of Sports Selector.

Now that they were sitting down, it was going

to be even harder. She had always thought of the tables in the food court as small, but this one felt like Mount Everest now that she was planning on kissing the boy on the other side of it.

I'll practically have to flip over it to get to him! she thought.

'Are you OK?' Jackson asked.

'Huh?' Olivia replied. 'I mean, yes, I'm fine.'

Now, should I go over the French fries or around the ketchup bottle? Olivia wondered.

'Are you feeling faint?' Jackson was watching her closely. 'You seem to be swaying.'

'Ha!' Olivia tried to laugh nonchalantly and wave away his concern, but she knocked over the salt and pepper shakers and sent them flying. 'Everything's great!'

You can't be happy that I'm going to kiss Garrick before you! Olivia thought. *So why don't you kiss me and make this all so much easier?*

She placed her hands on the table, lifted herself slightly off her chair, leaned across and . . . head-butted the tray of cakes and sodas being carried by the waitress who was bringing over the rest of their order.

It didn't hurt, but everything went flying with an embarrassing clatter and smash. Jackson was doused with soda and Olivia had cake splattered all over her white-and-yellow sweater.

'Oh my goodness, I'm so sorry,' she said to Jackson and to the waitress.

The waitress grabbed them some napkins and Olivia wished she could disappear into the palm fronds behind her. 'Hey – aren't you Jackson Caulfield?'

Covered in sticky soda, poor Jackson gave a weak smile. 'Yup, that's me!' Then he had to sign one of the napkins for the waitress.

'I'd better head home and take a shower,'

Jackson said, after the waitress had skipped off to show her friends.

'Yes, yes, of course,' Olivia stuttered, her cheeks colouring. All she really wanted to say was, *Kiss me, you fool!*

He gave her an awkward hug goodbye and left.

'That could not have gone any worse,' Olivia said to no one, burying her head in her hands.

🦇   🦇   🦇

'Horse-riding is much more glamorous than I realised,' Ivy decided, looking at herself from all angles in the mirror. Rebecca had given her a pair of tight-fitting black 'jodhpurs', along with calf-high leather boots. 'I could definitely rock this look, as long as the horse is not a required accessory.'

'Don't worry, Ivy,' Olivia said. She was wearing a similar outfit in beige and white, and had been bouncing on the bed with excitement while Ivy was getting dressed. 'It's going to be great!'

It was Saturday and they were back at Rebecca's ranch in Beldrake, bright and early in the morning, for Ivy's first-ever riding lesson. She'd reluctantly left her mom's diary up in the bedroom, getting Olivia to promise that they would have a look at it as soon as they got back.

Rebecca poked her head in the room. 'You girls ready?' she asked in her soft drawl. 'We need to be done by eleven.'

She had told them when they arrived that the ranch had taken a last-minute booking for a group trail ride – one of the many ways she supported all the horses – and the guests would be here at noon. 'There'll be tons of beginners, so once we show Ivy the basics, you girls can come on the trail ride, too,' Rebecca had said.

Ivy wasn't convinced. But here she was, dressed exactly like she'd been horse-riding forever. She took a deep breath. 'I'll try anything once.'

The three of them clattered down the stairs and into the stable.

Ivy tried not to be scared, or scary, but the horses started shuffling away from her and snorting.

'Maybe I should wait outside?' she asked hopefully.

Rebecca gave her a sympathetic look. 'OK. I'll tack up for you. Let's just find you a good helmet.'

Ivy tried on several in the tackroom until Rebecca was satisfied, then she went to wait outside the stable. When Rebecca and Olivia came out, they were leading Coco, Honey and a horse that Ivy hadn't met before named Topic. She was light brown with a black mane, tail and legs, and she had a white patch on her forehead.

'She's gentle and very tolerant,' Rebecca said.

You mean huge, Ivy thought.

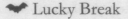

Rebecca showed her how to hold the reins, to lead her.

'Hold them right here, under her chin and keep your arm extended, so she has room to walk beside you.'

Ivy gulped and grasped the leather reins. She looked into Topic's huge eyes and thought, *Please don't freak out!*

Topic snorted and walked on, practically leading Ivy instead of the other way around. Ivy walked across the dirt and gravel towards the ring, feeling a little short of breath to be so close to such a strong creature.

So far, so good, Ivy thought.

Ivy stepped into the riding ring that was encircled by a white-painted fence. Despite the sunny day and clear blue sky, all she could think about was the headless horseman, thundering through the dark after his victims on his terrifying horse.

'Great job!' Rebecca said, with a big smile. 'How did that feel?'

'Uh . . . not as bad as I thought,' Ivy said. But walking next to a horse was one thing. She was dreading what was coming next.

'Oh, good,' Rebecca said. 'Time to mount up!'

Ivy gave a weak smile.

'You'll be fine,' said Olivia. 'Just think of her like a motorcycle.'

Ivy had always wanted to ride a big black motorcycle, dressed all in leathers. Maybe this wouldn't be so different. She would just be higher up, on a living creature that might choose to throw her to the ground.

'Olivia will hold Topic's head to keep her straight and I'll be right here to help you,' Rebecca said. Olivia spoke steadily to Topic as Ivy tried to build up courage. 'First, take the reins in your left hand and, with the same hand, grab a lock of mane.'

'Really?' Ivy said, cautiously following her instructions. 'Won't it hurt her?'

'No, no,' Rebecca said. 'You won't be putting your weight on it. Now, put your left foot in this stirrup. Grab the saddle here with your right hand.' Rebecca patted the back of it. 'Ready?'

No, no, no! Ivy wanted to scream, but she forced herself to nod.

'On the count of three, swing your right leg over. Try to land gently and not hit the horse with your leg.' Rebecca smiled, and the thought flashed in Ivy's mind that this would be just the moment to have her mom here. 'You can do it.'

Ivy closed her eyes.

'One, two, THREE!' Rebecca and Olivia counted together.

Ivy hauled herself up and swung her leg over.

When she opened her eyes, she was amazed to be sitting in the saddle.

'Oh my darkness,' she breathed.

Topic shifted her weight underneath her and Ivy felt a rush of adrenaline. She had done it! She was riding a horse! Well, OK, technically it was sitting still on a not-moving horse, but she never thought she'd get this far. Then she looked at the ground and realised she was pretty high up.

Gulp.

'Perfect!' Rebecca called up. 'Olivia, you mount up and we'll go on a little walk.'

Olivia got up on Honey easily, and Ivy felt better having her sister at the same height.

Rebecca started to lead Topic around the ring, and Ivy was amazed. Topic didn't seem to mind her at all. Ivy had no idea what to do or how to control her, but the horse hadn't bolted or freaked out. The steady rhythm of her plodding was soothing.

Ivy felt her heart race. She had a slightly different view of the farm. Suddenly the disapproving chickens seemed smaller and the dark wooden stable didn't look so imposing.

'I'm letting go now,' Rebecca said. 'Use the reins to point her nose in the direction you want her to go.'

Ivy felt the leather strap in her palm.

Can it really be that easy? she wondered. She pulled a little to the left and Topic obeyed.

'Wow,' Ivy breathed.

Hank and John, the stable hands, were watching from just outside the fence and applauded her.

'Go, Ivy!' John called. 'Ride 'em, cowgirl!'

'See what I mean?' Olivia called from just behind.

Ivy nodded. Suddenly, instead of demon

horses, she could imagine racing along green fields on Black Beauty . . .

'Told you I'd never failed to find a horse for a rider!' Rebecca said.

But just then, Topic tossed her head and side-stepped. Ivy hadn't done anything. 'Wh-what?'

Topic whinnied and pawed at the ground.

'Steady,' Rebecca's voice came from somewhere to the side, but Topic was already starting to buck. 'Steady!'

Ivy panicked; her mouth went dry and it felt hard to breathe. 'What do I do?' she shouted, pulling on Topic's reins as she bounced up and down.

'Stay calm!' called Rebecca. 'Steady, Topic!'

With one loud whinny, Topic reared up and Ivy couldn't hold on. She was falling. She landed with a thud on her side and cried out, feeling a shooting pain in her ankle.

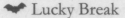

'Ivy!' Olivia was at her side in a moment, while Rebecca grabbed on to Topic, who was still spooking.

Ivy tried to control herself, but tears streamed down her cheeks.

'I'm just not meant to do this,' Ivy said to Olivia.

Her sister didn't say anything and gave her a huge hug.

'Are you OK?' Rebecca had handed Topic's reins to Hank, who had rushed over.

'My ankle,' Ivy said.

Topic gave an apologetic whinny as Hank led her back across the yard.

Rebecca carefully removed Ivy's boot and looked at her ankle. 'It doesn't seem broken. Can you stand on it?'

Ivy stood up and put her weight on it. It hurt but wasn't unbearable.

'I think it's just a little sprain,' Rebecca said. 'I'm so sorry – I should have stayed closer. You just seemed as natural as your sister.'

Ivy sniffled. 'I think me and horses don't go together.'

'Don't say that,' Rebecca said gently. 'I know that was scary, but it wasn't anything you did that spooked Topic.'

Ivy didn't believe her.

'Look.' Rebecca pointed to the edge of the ring near where Ivy had been riding a moment before. A mother duck and her three ducklings were waddling under the fencing.

'Topic is scared of ducklings?' Ivy asked, baffled. It might have been funny if she hadn't wanted it to be true so much.

'I know it sounds unlikely, but horses can get scared of lots of things,' Rebecca replied. 'Listen, let's get you inside to put that foot up.

We can try again another time.'

Ivy dusted herself down. She had tried horse-riding once and, as far as she was concerned, once was enough. As she limped back to the farmhouse, Ivy had to face the fact that she would never be a horsewoman like her mother.

Ivy sat on the porch swing, with her leg up and her notebook on her lap. She was trying to write a sonnet for English class but wasn't getting very far. She hadn't even had a chance to look at her mother's diary before Olivia had gone off with Rebecca, Hank and John on the trail ride.

Ivy was stuck at the farmhouse with a bruised ankle. They wouldn't be back for hours, so she'd sent a text to Brendan: *Cowgirl sings the blues. Could use city boy to help change her tune.*

Brendan had texted back right away: *Mounting my iron steed. Giddy up.*

Finally, she saw the little cloud of dust coming up the long driveway.

She wanted to run to greet him, but all she could manage was a few limping steps. Brendan put his brakes on, skidding in a half-circle to a stop in the yard.

Before he said anything, he held up his phone on full volume, playing 'I Wear My Sunglasses at Night'.

'No more cowgirl blues, please,' said Brendan. Then he grabbed her in a big hug.

'Careful of my ankle!' Ivy squealed, but she was so happy to see him.

Brendan scooped her up and carried her back to the porch. He sat her on the swing pillows and squeezed in next to her. She told him what had happened. 'I'm sorry you got hurt,' he said, 'but I'm very impressed that you were up on a horse in the first place.'

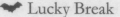

'It was going pretty well, actually,' Ivy said, rocking gently, 'until the Duckling Incident.'

Brendan chuckled. 'You must be pretty determined to connect to your mom if you got up on a horse.'

'That's exactly the problem,' Ivy replied. 'Even my dad can handle a horse. I'm clearly the black sheep of the family.'

'Nothing wrong with that,' Brendan said. 'You look good in black.'

'Yeah, but, what if . . .' Ivy had been thinking about it all morning. 'What if she was alive? What if she wouldn't get me?'

Brendan stopped her in mid-swing. 'Don't be silly, Ivy. You would be her daughter and she would love you. Besides, she obviously liked black because she loved your dad. Now, I want to see these terrifying ducklings.' Brendan pulled Ivy to her feet and grinned. 'Feel free to lean on me, if you need support.'

Ivy led him slowly over to the pond. The three fluffy yellow ducklings were quacking along behind their mother — a happy family in an orderly line.

Ivy sighed. That was just never going to be her family.

She heard a horse whicker from inside the barn.

'I thought all the horses were on a cattle drive,' Brendan said.

'All but Lucky,' Ivy replied. 'And it was a trail ride.'

'Isn't Lucky your mom's horse?' Brendan asked.

Ivy nodded.

Brendan looked at her. 'Do you want to go in?'

Ivy thought about it for a moment. Lucky hadn't shied away from her when they first met, and Rebecca insisted that the reason Topic was upset was the ducklings. Maybe she could go and

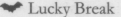

talk to Lucky. With Brendan by her side, she felt safe. 'Let's do it.'

They stepped into the cool barn, the smell of hay filling her nostrils as they clomped across the wooden floorboards. Lucky neighed from the back stall.

Very, very carefully, Ivy approached the stable door. Lucky poked his head out to see who it was and tossed his head.

'He's saying hello,' said Brendan.

Ivy remembered Olivia whispering to the horses and decided to try it herself.

'Hi Lucky,' she said quietly. 'I won't be afraid of you if you won't be afraid of me.'

Brendan stayed next to her as she reached her hand out to touch his muzzle.

Lucky stood still, his tail swishing. He seemed to be waiting for something.

Ivy glanced at the photos of her mom on

the wall. In one, her mom had her arm around Lucky, in a hug. 'If I hug Lucky,' Ivy whispered to Brendan, 'then it's almost like I'm hugging my mom.'

Ivy took a deep breath. She was going to get closer. She grabbed a rope off a nearby peg and pulled open the stable door. She walked down Lucky's left side, running her hand down his beautiful white neck. He didn't seem to mind at all. She clipped the lead rope on to his halter and took hold on his left, just like she had with Topic.

Lucky took a step out into the aisle, then another.

'He's beautiful,' said Brendan.

Ivy nodded, relaxing her grip on the rope a little, as Lucky walked out of his stable on his own.

'Wait, wait,' Ivy said to the horse. 'Don't go. We're not leaving.'

But Lucky seemed to think it was his turn for

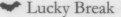

a walk. Ivy knew she couldn't handle him outside the stable.

'Uh oh,' Ivy whispered. 'I probably shouldn't have opened the door.'

Ivy fought back the panic. How was she going to get Lucky back in his stall? She pulled on the rope, trying to get Lucky to turn around. 'Lucky,' she sing-songed. 'Come back this way.'

She tried to hold on to his lead, but as she reached out, he backed up into the wall. Ivy shuffled one way and Brendan shuffled the other, trying to keep the horse contained. But Lucky didn't like it.

He whinnied and reared up, eyes rolling in his head as he pulled the rope right out of Ivy's hand.

She scrambled to get it back and Brendan did, too, but that only made things worse. Lucky shook his head and reared up, just inches away from Ivy.

She staggered back and tripped, only just managing to roll out of the path of his trampling hooves as he bolted. Her hair got in her face and she shouted, 'Lucky, wait!' as he galloped towards the stable door.

She scrambled to her feet, pain shooting through her ankle, only to see Lucky streaking across the ranch, towards the trees. This time there wasn't anyone to bring him back.

'Oh no, what have I done?' Ivy said, starting to cry.

Chapter Eight

Olivia was leading the group of visitors, while Rebecca pointed out the features of the trail and helped anyone who needed encouragement. Olivia loved riding Honey and the crisp, sunny day was perfect for the tour along the river and through the pine trees.

Rebecca had told her just to follow the green arrows, which was easy enough, and after a good two-hour ride, past a beautiful mini-waterfall, they were back at the ranch. Olivia had had plenty of time to think about Operation Smooch being a total failure so far. She couldn't believe

Jackson hadn't kissed her yet! Ivy thought he was waiting for the right moment, but it had better come along soon! *Or I'll have to kiss Garrick first!* thought Olivia with a shudder.

As she turned Honey towards the stable, she saw Ivy and Brendan waving frantically at her. She urged Honey into a trot and pulled her short when they got close.

Ivy's face was streaked with tears and Brendan looked more grave than usual.

Olivia dismounted right away. 'What's wrong?'

'Lucky,' Ivy gasped out. 'Lucky escaped!'

'Oh no!' Olivia whirled around to look in the direction that Ivy was pointing, into the woods.

A domestic horse out in the wild could be really vulnerable, Olivia knew. Especially one as old as Lucky.

'Aunt Rebecca!' she called across the yard.

Hank and John were leading the visitors back

to the stables and Rebecca rode over. 'What's happened?' she asked, keeping tight control over Admiral, who was prancing.

'It was all my fault,' Brendan put in. 'I left Lucky's stable door open. He ran away into the woods over there.'

Olivia glanced at Ivy, and she looked utterly crushed. Olivia wondered if there was more to the story than Brendan was letting on.

'How long ago?' Rebecca demanded.

'About half an hour,' Ivy said, fresh tears rolling down her face.

Rebecca looked down on Brendan from Admiral's back, like a general looking down on an army deserter. 'I think it's time you went home.'

Olivia felt awful. She knew Brendan wouldn't have done anything like that on purpose. Ivy started sobbing, and Brendan whispered something to her.

'I'm really sorry this has happened, Ms Kendall, and I hope you find Lucky soon.' He hugged Ivy tightly and then rode away on his bike.

'John and Hank will get the rest of the horses in and I'll go looking right away,' Rebecca said. 'I hope he hasn't gone far. Olivia, can you help?'

Olivia nodded.

'What can I do?' Ivy said. 'I have to help somehow.'

Rebecca tossed Ivy her cell phone. 'Call everyone in my phonebook and tell them what's happened. Anyone who can help, will, I'm sure.' She gave Ivy a sympathetic look. 'Ivy, don't beat yourself up over this. You're not to blame.' Then she rode away to the group.

'Don't worry,' Olivia said to Ivy. 'We'll find him.' She turned to mount Honey again but Ivy caught her arm.

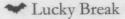

'It wasn't Brendan,' Ivy confessed. 'It was me.'

Olivia sucked in her breath. 'It doesn't matter now,' she replied. 'He'll be OK.'

The thought of Lucky alone out there in the woods made Olivia's heart ache. Ivy nodded and limped to the porch swing, clutching the phone like a lifeline. Olivia swung her leg over Honey and rode over to where Rebecca was briefing Hank and John.

Rebecca called out to the grey-haired, flannel-clad visitors, 'Thank you all very much for coming. I hope you enjoyed yourselves.' Then she said more quietly, 'Let's go, Olivia.'

They rode hard to the woods, where Ivy had pointed and then slowed down, looking for signs.

'This way,' Rebecca said. 'Where those branches are broken.'

The horses picked their way through the

trees, their hooves crackling the leaves and twigs underfoot.

'There are some positives,' said Rebecca, breaking the nervous silence. 'It's not winter any more, and Lucky wasn't fully tacked. It would be much worse if he had reins that could get caught on branches. He's a smart horse and knows the area very well.'

It wasn't much to believe in, but it made Olivia feel a tiny bit better.

'Horses like people and familiar things,' Rebecca went on. 'If he smells horses he knows or hears my voice, he might come to us.'

Olivia patted Honey on the neck. 'I'm glad you're here, then.' She'd only ridden her a few times but already she loved the horse. She could only imagine what Rebecca must be feeling for Lucky.

Olivia pushed a branch away from her face.

'I feel so awful. If we had never come –'

'Don't say that,' Rebecca said. 'You two are all the family I have left and having you here has been wonderful. But that Brendan boy . . .'

Olivia was torn. She wouldn't betray her sister's trust and tell the truth about how Lucky got out, but she couldn't let Rebecca think bad of him. 'Brendan is a really good person,' Olivia said. 'He's perfect for Ivy and treats her so well.' *Not to mention that he's really brave and loyal for taking the blame*, Olivia thought.

'Humph.' Rebecca changed the subject. 'I think I've lost the trail.'

They had emerged on to one of the many paths in the woods. It followed a high fence, and there were too many hoofprints to know which were Lucky's.

'What do we do now?' Olivia wanted to know.

'We should keep riding for a little while, and

then go back to see what group efforts we can coordinate.'

Olivia nodded.

She would do whatever it took to find Lucky – for Rebecca and for her bio-mom, but most importantly, for her sister.

🦇　　　🦇　　　🦇

'It will have to do for now.' Ivy closed her laptop sadly.

She'd been trawling the internet for advice on lost horses, and she'd found some great websites.

One woman had managed to convince the local police academy to run training exercises in the woods when she'd lost her horse and someone else had got the recreational pilot's club in the area to do a rota of flyovers. Ivy was willing to do anything to help find Lucky and she planned to start making phone calls first thing in the morning.

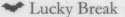

'You're doing everything you can,' Olivia offered.

Olivia looked dishevelled after five hours of searching. Ivy had spent her time phoning everyone that Aunt Rebecca knew and organising a search party of thirty people for first light tomorrow.

'I have never felt so wretched.' Her ankle throbbed and it felt like her legs were made of lead as she stood up to change into her bat-patterned pyjamas.

'It wasn't your fault,' Olivia replied with a pained expression. 'Don't blame yourself.'

'There is no one else to blame,' Ivy said. 'Brendan shouldn't have said he'd done it. I'm so lucky to have him – even if Aunt Rebecca doesn't think so.'

Olivia nodded. 'She just needs to get to know him.'

'Except now she'll never let him set foot on her property again,' Ivy replied.

I've messed everything up, Ivy thought. *I'm definitely not my mother's daughter.*

She thought about her mother's journal, lying wrapped up on top of the dresser. It was almost like she didn't deserve to read it any more.

As she laid down on the floor, wishing she was at home in her coffin, Ivy drifted off, to dream of a white horse running in the moonlight.

🦇　　　🦇　　　🦇

Back in Franklin Grove five days later, the twins were upset to hear that Lucky was still missing.

They had phoned Aunt Rebecca every day for updates, but there were no new leads. Now Olivia had to put him out of her mind. In less than an hour, it would be the grand opening of *Romezog and Julietron*. The entire cast was assembled backstage in all their metallic glory for a last-minute pep talk.

Aliens were perched on parts of the holodeck set, robots were scattered among the bizarre blue trees that Sophia had designed for the outdoor scenes. They were big spheres of Styrofoam stacked on top of each other. Everything was on wheels, ready to be whisked in and out by the stage crew at Ivy's command.

Camilla hopped up on to an alien sculpture from the party scene to address the group. 'You all look amazing and you've worked so hard. Our play is going to be in a galaxy of its own.' She looked very professional, dressed in a black suit with a moon rock necklace. 'Special praise goes to Sophia Hewitt for the incredible costumes and to Garrick for all the extra time he put in memorising his lines.'

Olivia had butterflies in her stomach that had

mutated into alien creatures that threatened to burst out of her and do a little dance on the table. Opening night meant no more air-kissing. This was it.

'And remember: yorg zup fandiot.' Camilla saluted and strode away.

'What on earth does that mean?' Olivia asked Jackson, who looked like a real cyborg in his metal and wires.

Jackson shrugged. 'Probably Martian for "Break a leg".'

Olivia giggled. 'I hope not! Can you imagine how funny Garrick would look writhing around even more than he already does!'

She glanced at her Romezog, who was sitting in the corner on a silver four-poster bed from Juliteron's bedroom scenes with his head in his hands – all ten of them.

That doesn't look good, Olivia thought.

'Thirty minutes until curtain,' Ivy called, in stage-manager mode. There were dark shadows under her eyes from worrying about Lucky. 'Doors are now open and the audience are taking their seats.'

Charlotte stomped past with Sophia chasing after her. 'I will *not* wear another pillow!'

Garrick didn't even look up.

'Just give me a minute,' Olivia said to Jackson and headed over to Garrick. She stood in front of him and said, 'I hope I don't regret asking, but what's wrong?'

'I can't find my itching powder,' he said, still staring at the floor. 'Without it, I can't do this.'

'What do you mean by "this"?' Olivia asked, worry creeping in.

'This!' He threw his many arms out wide, indicating the whole production. 'Be Romezog.'

Olivia's heart dropped into her knee-high gold

boots. If Garrick wouldn't take the stage, then there was no show!

'Don't say that,' Olivia said. 'The show must go on!'

'I can't,' he whined at her. 'The only reason I got the part was because of the itching. Now I won't get my kiss.' Garrick looked like a wreck. 'And I had all this extra stuff planned at the end, too.'

Olivia didn't know what to make of the extra stuff, but she knew she didn't want him to call off the performance. *You can't do* Romeo and Juliet *without Romeo . . . or Romezog,* she thought.

'You don't need the powder,' Olivia said. 'Just act it. Remember what it felt like and pretend.'

Garrick looked confused. 'Pretend to itch?'

Olivia suppresed the urge to beat him with his

goggly eyes. 'Yes, pretend. You are supposed to be acting, after all.'

'Maybe . . .' Garrick stood up.

Jackson came over. 'Break a leg,' he said to Garrick, flashing a grin at Olivia.

'Enough with the jealousy, man,' Garrick said.

'No, no,' Jackson replied. 'That's how they say "good luck" in the theatre.'

'Oh, well, uh, thanks, but I can't go on.' Garrick shuffled his feet.

'Are you kidding?' Jackson said. 'You are the most convincing alien octopus that has ever graced the stage.'

'Absolutely!' Olivia added, hoping she sounded like she meant it.

Garrick looked suspicious.

'I'm serious,' Jackson said. 'You own that role. Be confident, man. Be strong!' Garrick started to nod along. 'You are Romezog, and you will have your Julietron!'

'You're right, Jay Jay,' Garrick said, punching Jackson on the arm. 'I will have her, won't I?' He winked at Olivia and made a clicking noise. 'See *you* on stage, baby.' Garrick stood up from the bed and sauntered off.

Olivia hit Jackson gently. 'Did you have to use me as bait?'

'Hey,' Jackson said, leaning in so close that she could see the flecks in his blue eyes. 'A kiss with you would get anyone to do anything.'

Olivia shivered and clutched one of the posters of the bed behind her. She had tried so many ways to corner him and kiss him this past week, but something had always gotten in the way. *Is he saying that he wants to kiss me?* Olivia hoped so. She had just minutes to kiss him before Garrick got there first.

'I would happily get stabbed with a retractable

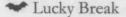

sword for you,' Jackson grinned, referring to his death in the play.

Olivia smiled back.

'You are an amazing Juliet and a wonderful actress,' he said quietly, stepping even closer.

The noise of swords clashing backstage, Charlotte complaining, props being moved around – they all faded away as Jackson took her face in his hands. Was it finally going to happen?

'And an awesome girlfriend,' he whispered.

She closed her eyes and felt his breath on her face. Her heart was pounding.

'Fifteen minutes!' shouted Ivy, making Olivia jump.

Jackson took a step away from her.

No! Olivia thought. *Come back! So close!*

Then Garrick sauntered over and pressed something into her hand. Baffled, Olivia saw a wrapped-up mint. 'It's for later,' he mock-whispered.

Olivia wanted to scream, but all she could do was grit her teeth. Her last chance to kiss Jackson was ruined – and now there was no escape.

Garrick Stevens was going to be her first kiss.

Chapter Nine

Ivy looked out across the lobby of the theatre where friends, family and what seemed like every girl under the age of sixteen within a twenty-mile radius were milling around.

One girl with blonde pigtails was flipping through the specially printed programmes. 'What do you mean he isn't Romeo? Isn't this *Romeo and Juliet*?'

Her black-haired friend pointed to a page. 'It says here that he's some kind of cyborg.'

'Well,' replied Pigtails, 'I don't care if it's science fiction or science class, as long as I've got a seat up close! I didn't buy this ticket off eBay to sit at the back.'

Ivy rolled her eyes, but at least having Jackson in the cast helped Camilla's directorial debut become the fastest sell-out production in Franklin Grove Middle School's history.

But the only two audience members she cared about right now were obviously not following instructions. They were late.

She looked past the dolled-up girls and spotted a solo figure in a simple, dashing black suit and a mandarin-collared white shirt, almost hiding behind a pot plant.

'Dad!' Ivy shouted.

He was staring in completely the wrong direction. Ivy only had fifteen minutes to round him up, find Aunt Rebecca, get them to their reserved seats *and* be backstage before the curtain went up.

'VIP number one spotted,' she reported to Sophia over the headphones. 'VIP number two, unaccounted for.'

'Check,' Sophia replied. 'Twelve minutes.'

A red sweater dress caught Ivy's attention. It was Rebecca on the opposite side of the lobby, by the ladies' room.

Ivy marched over to her dad. 'Hi, Dad, not much time, got to keep moving,' she said in one breath.

'OK, Ivy.' He stumbled along, trying to keep up. 'All going well backstage?'

'We are on target,' Ivy confirmed. 'Except for you and Aunt Rebecca.' She gave him a pointed look.

'My apologies –' he began.

'No time!' Ivy cut him off. By then, they had reached the opposite corner of the lobby. 'Aunt Rebecca, it is lovely to see you; you look so nice; please come this way.'

'Goodness,' Rebecca said. She'd matched knee-high boots with her red sweater dress and an embossed brown leather belt. 'You are efficient!'

'I've saved seats for you,' Ivy replied, pushing open the glass doors, manoeuvring past the people taking their seats at the back of the theatre and leading them down the centre aisle of the school theatre.

'You are there,' she said to Mr Vega and he obediently moved in to sit down next to Brendan. 'And you are there.'

'There?' A flicker of awkwardness flashed across Aunt Rebecca's face.

Ivy realised what she'd done. She should have 'accidentally' saved them separate seats. Rebecca wasn't exactly long-lost friends with her dad and Brendan was probably on her least-favourite-person list at the moment. But it was too late now. The show was sold out and she didn't have time to move things around.

'Ten minutes,' came Sophia through the headset.

Ivy put on a bright face, hoping to get away as fast as she could. 'Yup, right there. Best seats in the house.'

'Uh, thanks,' Rebecca replied. She smoothed her dress and sat down next to Mr Vega. 'Good evening,' she said stiffly.

'Good evening,' he replied.

She didn't even acknowledge Brendan.

'I hope you enjoy the show!' Ivy wanted to smack her own forehead, but there wasn't even time to do that.

As she hurried up the steps, she heard Mr Vega go straight to the subject Ivy was hoping to avoid tonight.

'Any news about Lucky?' he asked.

Ivy knew there wasn't. She'd been texting all day and all week. They hadn't found any trace of Lucky.

Ivy forced all thoughts of the horse out of her mind. She had to get through the show and then she could think about it.

'Ivy, dear!' exclaimed a voice in front of her. It was Olivia's mom.

Mrs Abbott gave Ivy a hug, and Mr Abbott grinned at her.

'We're so excited about tonight,' Mrs Abbott said. She was wearing an elegant emerald dress with a silver clutch. 'Olivia has been practising so hard!'

'And she tells us you've been keeping everything running smoothly,' said Mr Abbott, in a dark grey suit with a black tie.

Ivy smiled. 'Thanks.' The Abbotts always

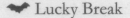

cheered her up. 'I've got to run; curtain's up soon.'

'The obstacle is the path,' Mr Abbott said and bowed to her.

Ivy instinctively bowed back then hurried up the steps.

Olivia peeked through the wing, stage right, careful to make sure no one in the audience could see her.

Jackson was standing on a holodeck control board above Garrick and making the goggly eyes of his costume bounce wildly. 'And in this state she gallops night by night, through lovers' brains, and then they dream of love . . .'

He was giving the famous Queen Mab speech. It started out teasing Romeo about being in love but then turned into a rage against the alien–robot feud and how everyone was obsessed with all the wrong things.

194

The audience, including Mr Vega and her parents, were watching, enthralled.

Who would have thought Mercutio as a cyborg could make so much sense? Olivia thought. Jackson was so good, exaggerating just the right phrases to make the meaning clear. No one could have done Merc-X88 better, Olivia knew, but that didn't stop her wishing that he'd been cast as Romeo instead.

As he danced off stage, on his way to the robots' feast, the audience burst into applause. Olivia felt her pulse start to race. He was coming straight towards her and he had such an exhilarated smile on his face.

'I was hoping to run into you,' he whispered and pulled her away from the other actors leaving the stage, into the darkness of the curtains.

Olivia knew there was a brief scene with butler robots before she had to go on. Was it enough time to kiss him? 'You were?' she said, looking into his silver-coloured face.

'Yes, I just wanted . . .' Jackson trailed off.

'Julietron!' hissed Ivy from somewhere nearby. 'Cue Julietron with the Capulets!'

Just one second, Olivia thought. *Please!*

But Jackson was already backing off. 'You're doing so great,' he whispered. 'Get back out there and knock 'em dead.'

Olivia wasn't sure her heart could take any more almost-kisses. She knew she was supposed to be on stage, but it was time to take matters into her own hands. She was just going to kiss him – now or never.

She took a step forwards.

'Olivia!' Ivy's voice stopped her in her tracks. 'Your cue!'

'Arg!' Olivia said, peeling away from Jackson to rush on stage into a melee of metallic masks

196

and actors jerking about like mechanical puppets.

The fates were against Romeo and Juliet, Olivia thought as she moved around to the thumping synthetic music, *and they are determined not to let me kiss my boyfriend!*

🦇   🦇   🦇

In every break during the rest of the performance, Olivia tried to find Jackson again, but the closest she came was a glimpse across the backstage area while she was rushing for a costume change. Operation Cyborg Smooching had failed.

Now, Olivia was lying as still as she could while Garrick twitched around the cryogenic tomb she was on top of, performing his last monologue in the scene where Romezog arrives to find Julietron apparently dead, not knowing that she has been injected with an internal cryogenesis solution that gives the appearance of death.

'Death, that hath suck'd the honey of thy breath, hath had no power yet upon thy beauty,' he was saying. Olivia was impressed by Garrick – he had only missed a line or two throughout the whole show. The audience was silent, and Olivia hoped they were feeling the building climax of the tragedy.

With each line Garrick spoke, she knew it came closer and closer to the end where she would have to kiss him – and there was nothing to convince her that it would be anything but the grossest moment of her life.

She would have to make sure she didn't vomit in front of everyone.

Garrick climbed on to the tomb with her and accidentally whacked her in the face with one of his costume's arms. Olivia struggled not to react; she was supposed to be in system malfunction mode.

'Eyes, look your last!' Garrick was building up to the end. 'Arms, take your last embrace!' With that, he whacked her again with an octopus arm.

He lay down beside her and drank a purple vial of Astrolaudanum. Garrick gasped and choked and hammed up his death for at least a minute too long, then went silent.

That was Olivia's cue to wake up.

'What's here?' she said. She was pretending it was Jackson that she was looking at, imagining what it might feel like if that was him. 'A cup clos'd in my true love's hand? Poison, I see, hath been his timeless end.'

She reached up to the back of her head to turn herself off and when she slumped on top of Garrick, Olivia heard several people sniffling in the audience – they were crying!

She had to bite the inside of her cheeks not to smile broadly.

Of course, they don't know what's coming next, Olivia thought. This was not the end of their show. Camilla had written an extra scene where Olivia would have no choice but to kiss the beastly boy.

The lights turned red, green, blue and purple and the theatre filled with an electronic humming sound. On cue, Olivia and Garrick stood bolt upright as the audience gasped in astonishment. They knew this wasn't how the story of Romeo and Juliet went. Camilla's big rewrite was to have them come back to life after dying, to give them the happy ending Shakespeare denied them.

Garrick and Olivia looked at each other and continued the scene. Olivia had to raise her voice over a muttering that she thought might be a disapproving Mr Wagenbach.

'Sometimes, the fates do not stand for good people making mistakes,' Olivia intoned.

Oddly, there was a silence. *Has Garrick forgotten his next line?* Olivia wondered.

But then Garrick started up again. 'Thou lookest most delicious, my Julietron.'

What? Olivia knew that wasn't what he was supposed to say. It should have been something about the power of love.

'Cometh into my alien arms,' Garrick went on.

Olivia could see Ivy just off-stage frantically gesturing at Garrick to get back on script.

What is he up to? Olivia started to panic. *Is this the extra stuff he had planned? That fake Shakespeare sounds awful!*

'A taste, sweet Julietron, of your tinny flesh. Just one bite!'

Bite? Garrick leaned closer and Olivia saw that he was wearing a set of false vampire teeth! *When did he put those on?* He was trying to turn Camilla's sci-fi theme into a vampire one.

Olivia hopped off the tomb to get away from him and continued with the lines as Camilla wrote them, trying to force Garrick back on script. 'A peace between our races would serve the fates.'

'Who cares about peace? You're supposed to be mine!' Garrick advanced, his ten arms outstretched, trying to grab hold of Olivia.

She decided to buy herself some time, running away from Garrick. But she had to stay in character and run like a robot. Garrick chased her with his twitchy, itchy shuffle.

The both looked absolutely ridiculous.

She should have known, when it came down to it, they could not trust Garrick.

You are in so much trouble! Olivia thought. *When this mess is over, I am going to pluck your arms off one by one! And then Ivy and I – and Camilla – will bash you with them!*

Just as Garrick was about to catch her, someone shouted, 'Behold!'

Garrick froze.

Jackson, in only part of his Merc-X88 costume, leaped on stage from the wings. 'I thought my fate was sealed by that foul Tybalt,' he said, improvising much better Shakespeare than Garrick. 'Now it seems I am the cat with nine lives.'

'You cannot stop me,' Garrick muttered.

Jackson darted in front of him. 'Romezog, selfishness has consumed you. You must be banished from Veronova.'

Olivia saw Camilla pushing three supporting actors on stage to help Jackson restrain Garrick and haul him off, making it look like an arrest. He shouted the whole time that Romezog would return.

When the silence fell, Olivia realised that it

was just her and Jackson on stage, and that they had to end the play.

Jackson extended an arm and said, 'Will you take my hand, beautiful Julietron?'

Olivia wanted to rush across the stage to him, but she couldn't break character. She had to do her robot-walk across the stage.

But what are we going to do when I get there? Olivia wondered. *How can we end* Romezog and Julietron *without Romezog?*

Finally, Olivia reached him, and felt her heart threatening to bounce right out of her chest. Jackson had the same look on his face as when he had pulled her into the wings.

'May I kiss you?' Jackson asked.

In a rush, she realised that she was going to get her wish after all. *Not really how I imagined it, but it's super romantic all the same.*

It took everything Olivia had to nod like a

robot and not like a human in love.

As Jackson leaned in towards her, the theatre lights blacked out. Their first kiss was in complete darkness. A moment shared by only them.

Jackson pressed his lips against hers, and Olivia closed her eyes. It was soft and gentle, and sent a shiver down her spine like goosebumps.

A short pause later, there was thunderous applause and they broke apart. The lights came up, and the rest of the cast, with a grumpy-looking Garrick, joined them on stage for a bow.

Olivia held Jackson's hand as they bowed together and felt tingly with happiness. She knew she would never forget her first kiss.

Chapter Ten

'Nice save,' Ivy said to Jackson as the cast rushed backstage, buzzing with the excitement of the closing scene. 'I am going to *kill* Garrick.'

'Not if I get there first,' Olivia said.

Ivy chuckled. Garrick wouldn't stand a chance with the twins after him!

'Mission accomplished,' Sophia said, hurrying over from the wings and taking off her headphones.

'Was that . . . the lights? Was that you?' Olivia asked.

'Ivy's idea over the headphones, my execution,' Sophia admitted. 'Just in time, too.'

'I wanted you two to have a little privacy,' Ivy explained.

'Thank you,' Olivia said at the same time as Jackson.

Ivy could see that her sister was absolutely beaming – from the buzz of performing, or from finally getting that kiss with Jackson? Probably both.

Camilla burst into the green room, with an unreadable look on her face.

Uh oh, Ivy thought. Camilla had been so strict through all the rehearsals. What did she think of the chaos of her carefully constructed ending?

Camilla broke out in a huge smile. 'That was better than I could have ever imagined. Why didn't I think of putting Juliet with Mercutio?' She gave them both a hug. 'We're going to do the rest of the performances like that, as long as I can keep Garrick in check.'

By then, other cast members' families were flooding backstage, presenting everything from neon flower bouquets to boxes of gold-painted chocolates.

'Olivia!' called Mrs Abbott, waving from the curtains. 'Can we join you?'

'Of course.' Camilla waved them over. 'Your daughter is a genius!'

'We're so proud of you, honey,' Mrs Abbott said.

'And, ahem, Jackson you were, uh, very good, too.' Mr Abbott was having a hard time saying it.

Ivy saw her sister blush. It must have been weird for Mr Abbott to almost-witness his daughter's first kiss.

'Thanks so much for putting up with me,' Ivy overheard Camilla saying to Olivia.

'It was a great show,' Olivia replied. 'You are really a fantastic writer and director.'

'I agree,' said a familiar voice behind Ivy. It was Amy Teller – Ivy hadn't noticed her in the audience. She must have been right at the back.

'You whipped a motley crew into shape in three weeks and put on a very entertaining show.' Amy nodded her approval. 'I'll be keeping my eye on you, young lady. I'm always looking to make friends with talented people.'

Camilla blushed and Olivia clapped for her.

Ivy spotted her dad through the crowd, followed by Aunt Rebecca.

Rebecca smiled and waved, but thoughts of Lucky came rushing back and, suddenly, Ivy didn't feel like celebrating any more.

'I wasn't expecting to like the sci-fi version,' Mr Vega said to Camilla. 'But it really worked.'

Camilla grinned. 'Thank you.'

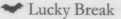

'And you, Olivia, were a wonderful Julietron,' he continued.

'I couldn't have said it better,' Aunt Rebecca said.

Ivy shared a look with Olivia. That might be the first time those two had ever agreed on anything.

Maybe it could be the beginning of the two of them finally getting along?

Ivy dropped her fork and it clattered on to her half-eaten plate of food.

'Sorry,' she murmured.

They were back at the ranch, silently hoping for any hint of news about Lucky. It had been a week since he'd escaped and there hadn't been any sign of him. How was he getting through the cold nights and was he OK without his medicine? *If only I'd never gone into that stable!* Ivy felt like she would never stop berating herself.

'It's been a hard week,' Rebecca said, to fill the silence. 'But I'm not giving up hope.'

Ivy felt as grey as the sky. Outside, the wind was blowing like a storm was coming.

During this lunch, there had already been three choruses of, 'It's not your fault, Ivy.' And it seemed there wasn't much else to say.

Once they were done with their mushroom salad, Olivia and Rebecca were planning to go out riding again. Ivy had nibbled a Vita Vamp bar in the bathroom just before lunch, but it had tasted sour.

Hank and John were already out there, searching. Ivy and Mr Vega would only be able to sit and wait.

Ivy picked at her food. She wouldn't want even a rare sirloin steak today. Her appetite was lost somewhere out there in the woods with Lucky.

'Lovely meal,' Mr Vega said, being polite. Of course, he'd much rather be sinking his teeth into a beef stir-fry or some Italian meatballs.

At least he's trying to get along with Rebecca, Ivy thought.

'Thank you,' Rebecca replied, but the conversation couldn't go any further. There just wasn't much to talk about that wasn't about Lucky.

The ringing phone cut through the silence and made Ivy jump.

Rebecca flew out of her chair to the phone on the wall, a hopeful look on her face. 'Yes, hello?' Ivy wanted to hear what was being said, until she saw her aunt's face fall. 'Yes, yes, it's OK. I understand.' Rebecca started sniffling. 'Thank you for trying.'

When she hung up, Rebecca leaned against the kitchen counter.

'That was Jerry Green, the local sheriff. He's

suspending the search by his department. They did a last sweep this morning, but there's nothing more they can do.' Rebecca slid down the wall and buried her head in her hands. 'I just have to accept that we're not going to find him.' Her voice was muffled.

Ivy couldn't take it any more. *I did this*, she thought. 'Excuse me,' she said.

Olivia made eye contact, asking if Ivy wanted company, but Ivy shook her head. She just wanted to be alone.

She rushed up the stairs and threw herself on the big quilt. The square she was lying on had a little blue embroidery – the initials S.K. This square was her mom's – that meant probably the whole quilt was.

I'm so stupid. Why did I even try to bond with Lucky? I'm not my mom. I'm not good with horses.

Ivy wiped her eyes and her black eyeliner

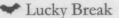

smeared across the back of her hand. She didn't even care.

She reached for her phone and called Brendan, but there was no answer. She tried a second time and then gave up, turning off her phone.

Maybe if Mom was here, she thought, *she would know what to do*. Ivy sat bolt upright. *But Mom is* sort of *here* . . .

She opened the desk drawer and took out the precious journal. *What if she wrote something about Lucky? Where they liked to ride to, where he might be.*

Ivy knew she had promised to look at it with her sister, but Olivia would understand. She tucked it under her arm, crept down the stairs, grabbed her black pea coat and went out into the muggy air. The spot where Lucky disappeared looked like a black hole in the tree line. Ivy knew that's where she should start.

'Who says I can't search on foot?' she said aloud.

She opened the journal and read as she walked, not really knowing where she was going.

Help me, Mom. Help Lucky.

She flicked through pages, catching words and phrases here and there, but there weren't many mentions of horses in the first pages. Finally a sentence caught her attention.

I just don't get why Rebecca is so obsessed with the horses, her mom had written.

Ivy stopped in her tracks. She couldn't believe what she was reading. *That can't be right!* Ivy thought. Her mom was horse-crazy. There were photos everywhere to prove it.

Ivy wracked her brain but realised that in all the journal entries she'd read so far, there hadn't been any mention of her mom riding horses, just Rebecca.

She kept reading and walking, stepping over gnarled tree-roots as she went.

They are beautiful, but – I'd never tell Rebecca this – they are scary. And there are so many things to remember to do. I think I'll never be a horsey person. Rebecca said that horses can sense your fear, and I think they can smell me a mile off. They always look like they want to run away from me.

Ivy was astounded. Her mom had the same problem that she had. Her mom wasn't a vampire, which could mean only one thing. *I inherited my fear of horses from her!* Ivy couldn't resist the spark of hope that lit up inside her. She had something in common with her mom, after all.

▾   ▾   ▾

Olivia scrubbed at the plate, even though she could see that it was already clean.

She was helping Aunt Rebecca wash up after lunch. Hank and John had come back, with no news except that they thought a heavy rainstorm was coming. Rebecca didn't think the trails would be safe, so she decided to wait until it passed to set out again.

The idea of washing the dishes was to take her mind off Lucky, but not much could. It was an awful thing for such a magnificent creature to be lost and alone, especially one as vulnerable as Lucky.

'Thank you for lunch,' Mr Vega said. 'I'll head back home now.'

'You are welcome,' Rebecca said, with none of the warmth she used when talking to the girls. She was courteous, as always, but that's as far as it went between the two of them.

Olivia gave her bio-dad a hug, and then he went to the bottom of the stairs. 'Ivy! Come and say goodbye; I'm heading home.'

There was no answer.

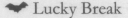

'Maybe she has her headphones on,' Olivia suggested. 'I'll just run up and check.'

Olivia went upstairs to their shared bedroom, opened the door and saw . . . an empty room.

'She's gone!' she called down the stairs. 'Ivy's gone!'

🦇   🦇   🦇

Ivy was entranced by the journal, reading as quickly as she could, glancing up only briefly to avoid being hit in the face by branches.

It's like everyone telling me to grow my hair and wear flowery dresses. Why do I have to look like everyone else?

Her mom talked about feeling less pretty than Rebecca, even though they looked almost exactly the same, and how sometimes she felt the extended family preferred Rebecca.

Ivy clutched the journal tightly.

There was a time when her mother felt like she didn't belong, too. But she didn't let it upset her, and she didn't change who she was. Ivy knew she must have inherited that from her mom, too.

She flicked on a few pages and saw entries about the pregnant horse, Lavender.

I've decided I want to have tons of kids when I grow up – like five.

Ivy's heart skipped a beat.

Lavender looks so huge. John says the foal will come any day now and he's said I can help, if I want to. I definitely do! I just hope it happens before we have to go back to school.

Ivy didn't know what exactly she was looking for but kept scanning the pages. After the entry about Lucky's difficult birth and choosing his name, there was a section about how Lucky liked being sung to.

I tried 'Raindrops Keep Falling on My Head' but that didn't work as well as 'American Pie'.

Ivy didn't really know either of those songs,

but if she ever managed to find Lucky, she could always try singing to him.

She looked back down at the journal and saw a fat raindrop splattered on the page. Then another.

Uh oh. Ivy realised it was about to rain and she had no idea where she was. She quickly closed the journal and tucked it into the large pocket inside her coat. She didn't want it to get wet.

She saw a clearing ahead through the trees and hurried there, raindrops plopping on the leaves at her feet. Then, she heard a shuffling coming from ahead, something like a creature.

Ivy froze and listened.

Then she heard a whinny.

Lucky? Ivy sprinted into the clearing to see a rickety wooden shack on the other side of a high fence.

Surely Lucky can't be in there, Ivy thought. The

fence was almost as tall as Ivy was, and Lucky would have had to jump over it.

She could hear a stomping and a snort. It had to be a horse.

Then, Ivy remembered what Rebecca had said – Lucky was a jumping champion. He could have jumped the fence!

Ivy hauled herself up the fence and had to swing her leg over, like she did to ride Topic. She jumped down carefully into the grassy field and hurried over to the shack.

Pulling open the door, Ivy wanted to weep with joy. It was Lucky!

'Lucky, I'm so sorry,' she said. 'But I'm going to get you home. Don't you worry.'

His lead had caught on a broken wooden board. Ivy noticed that there was a stack of old hay and a water butt that collected rain water from the roof that he had been surviving on. No one had thought to look here before because of the fence.

As Ivy went to free the lead, Lucky panicked. He starting rearing up, and Ivy knew she had to calm him down.

She sang the first thing that came into her head, which was the song Brendan had played for her on his phone: 'I Wear My Sunglasses at Night'.

It seemed to work. Lucky stopped pawing the air and his breathing slowed. Ivy kept singing and moved in to take his lead. She wasn't going to let it go this time.

She unhooked it from the board and led him out of the shack, into the light rain. Ivy didn't want to make Lucky jump the fence so she walked along it until she found a rusty gate. It creaked open and Lucky stepped through.

'Now, how to get home?' Ivy wondered,

but Lucky seemed to want to pull her off to the left.

Ivy looked where Lucky was heading and saw a clear trail marking.

'Yes!' Ivy said. 'Clever Lucky.'

Chapter Eleven

'What should we do?' Rebecca said, clearly distraught.

'I think she's gone looking for Lucky,' Olivia said. She knew her sister felt responsible and that Ivy wouldn't be able to sit around doing nothing.

'But she doesn't know her way around those woods!' Mr Vega declared. 'We have to find her.'

'We can't let Ivy get lost!' Olivia cried, her stomach doing a triple flip.

Just then, there was a clap of thunder.

'There's a storm coming,' Rebecca said. 'We've got to act fast.'

Knock, knock.

Someone was at the front door!

Olivia, Rebecca and Mr Vega rushed down the hall and Olivia flung open the door. It was Brendan, looking damp and worried. His black hair was sticking to his pale face and his boots were caked in mud.

'I had two missed calls from Ivy but now her phone is off.' He shivered on the porch. 'Her phone is never off. Something's wrong, so I got my parents to drop me here.'

Rebecca looked as stormy as the sky but didn't say anything.

Olivia was even more worried seeing the state he was in. 'Something is wrong. Ivy's missing.'

'Come in; come in,' Mr Vega said, while Rebecca stayed silent.

Brendan stepped into the hall and wiped his feet on the mat. 'I know I'm not exactly welcome,' he said to Rebecca, 'but I had to find out what was happening.'

'I can tell you what's happening,' Rebecca snapped, blocking his way down the hall. 'Because of you, my niece is wandering in unfamiliar woods looking for a lost and frightened horse with a storm on the way. You never should have been alone with Ivy in the stable.'

Olivia was stunned at Rebecca's outburst. They were all upset, but there was no reason to take it out on Brendan.

'Rebecca, please,' Mr Vega said. 'Brendan is a good kid; he's just worried.'

Brendan looked miserable at having caused all this tension.

'Of course you would defend him,' Rebecca snapped. 'He's just like you.'

Mr Vega took a step back. 'What does that mean?'

Rebecca's eyes flashed. 'It means he will take Ivy away from her family – just like you took Susannah.'

'Stop!' shouted Olivia. She couldn't take it any more.

Mr Vega's face was white with shock – even more than normal. 'Is that really what you've thought all these years? Rebecca . . .'

But as he took a step towards her, holding out his hand, the house was rattled by another huge thunderclap and the sky outside glowed from the lightning.

Brendan turned on his heel and ran at full speed into the woods. 'Ivy!' he shouted.

'Brendan!' yelled Mr Vega, but he was gone.

Olivia started to run after him but Mr Vega grabbed her by the shoulders. 'You are staying put. This is nearing crisis. We have two children out in the woods with a dangerous storm coming.'

He turned to Rebecca. 'No matter what you may think of me, we need to focus on that.'

Rebecca nodded mutely. Olivia wondered if she was realising that she had practically driven Brendan out into the storm. 'I'll call the sheriff.'

Olivia closed her eyes as another thunderbolt hit. *Please let everything be OK. Please!*

Ivy was struggling to see from all the water pouring down her face. She wasn't going to relax her grip on Lucky's lead for anything, which meant she only had one hand free to wipe the rain from her eyes.

'Stay dark; gonna block out the light. I wear my sunglasses at night.'

Ivy had sung the chorus about a hundred times but it kept Lucky and her steadily moving forwards along the trail, which was turning into a little stream.

Her coat was soaked and so were her jeans. Rain was dripping off Lucky's mane. Ivy had hoped the trail would lead them back to the ranch, but so far there hadn't been any sight of her aunt's home.

Then, an old barn came into view. It didn't look recently used, but it was shelter and would do until the storm calmed.

She led Lucky inside the empty building, singing the whole time. There were several leaks in the roof, so the floor was wet, but at least there was some shelter.

The heavy rain sounded like pebbles beating down on the rickety roof. Soon, Ivy started to shiver in the wet and cold.

'You must be cold, too,' she said to Lucky and the horse swung his head towards hear and nuzzled her shoulder.

Ivy was stunned. It was like Lucky was giving

her a hug. Carefully, still holding on to the lead with one hand, Ivy put her other arm around the white horse.

The thunder clapped and Lucky stiffened, so Ivy sang louder.

'Ivy?' came a muffled but familiar voice from outside.

'Brendan?' she called back.

'Ivy!' he shouted, sounding nearer and Lucky started getting skittish.

'Wait! Don't come in!' Ivy called, in between singing.

'What do you mean?' He was right outside now.

'I found Lucky and I'm scared he'll bolt if you frighten him.'

'But, Ivy, the barn's roof looks bowed,' Brendan said. 'It could collapse under the weight of all this water.'

Ivy looked at the little waterfalls coming

through the cracked roof and knew Brendan was right.

'OK, but I'm not leaving Lucky,' Ivy said. 'If you want to help, you have to sing.'

'Uh, what?'

'Sing something!'

'The itsy bitsy spider . . .' Brendan said and poked his head around the door. He was dripping wet, his black hair like tendrils on his pale skin.

Lucky eyed him warily. Ivy joined in, so they were singing together. 'Down came the rain . . .'

After a little while, Lucky calmed down and Ivy led him out with Brendan by her side.

'The farm is this way,' Brendan said, pointing down a small path Ivy was sure she would have missed. 'Out came the sun . . .'

'How did you know to come looking for me?' Ivy said.

'You called me but when I tried to call

back, your phone was off,' he replied. 'I knew something was wrong.'

The rain eased a little, but they kept singing. Ivy couldn't risk losing Lucky again. After a couple of bends in the path, Ivy saw the farmhouse through the trees. There were also the flashing lights of a police car.

Uh oh, Ivy thought.

As soon as they broke through the trees, the front door banged open and Olivia, her dad and Rebecca sprinted out to meet them, ignoring the rain.

'You found them!' Olivia cried to Brendan.

'Oh, Lucky!' said Rebecca, taking the lead from Ivy.

Mr Vega grabbed his two girls in a huge, damp hug.

A sheriff in a tan Stetson covered with plastic to keep off the rain followed. 'Glad everything is under control. I'll call the station.' He walked off to his car.

Rebecca had been examining Lucky. 'He's under-fed, but he looks fine. I'll just take him in and call the vet,' Rebecca said. 'Please, you all go inside and get warm. I'm going to check Lucky over.'

Olivia went inside and rushed upstairs for towels and a change of clothes for Ivy, while their dad made some hot chocolate. Ivy sank down on to a wooden chair, exhausted.

'You will never, never do anything like that again,' her dad said to Ivy, handing over a steaming mug. 'That means you, too, Brendan.'

Soon, Rebecca came into the kitchen, her arms across her chest.

'How did you find him?' she asked.

'I don't know really,' Ivy said. 'I was just wandering, and I found him in a shack behind a really high fence. He'd caught his lead on the shelter, so was stuck. But the thing that made me able to bring him back was Mom's journal.'

'A journal?' Mr Vega said.

'We found Mom's journal,' Olivia said as Ivy pulled it out, still dry.

'It said that she used to sing to Lucky, and so Brendan and I sang all the way home.'

Rebecca shot a look at Brendan. It wasn't as angry as before, but she still wasn't happy with his presence. Ivy took a deep breath. 'If Brendan hadn't come to find me, I don't know how I would have found my way home. I was completely lost. And . . .' Ivy had to say it. 'It wasn't Brendan that let Lucky escape. It was me. He just took the blame so that you wouldn't hate me.'

'I would never hate you!' Rebecca said, rushing over to give Ivy a hug. She finally met Brendan's eye. 'And it seems I misjudged you. I'm sorry, Brendan.'

Brendan nodded, his wet curls still dripping on to the towel. 'Don't worry about it.'

'And thank you, as well, for bringing my niece and my horse home.' It was awkward but Rebecca wrapped Brendan in a big hug.

'Can I . . .?' Mr Vega was staring at the journal.

Ivy looked at Olivia and knew that she was thinking the same thing.

'Of course,' Ivy replied and pushed it across the table to him.

They all gathered around and read a section about how Susannah loved Lucky but not all the manure she had to muck out.

They were all in stitches as Rebecca told the story of the first time Susannah mucked out Lucky's stall and ended up slipping in the mess.

Rebecca turned to Mr Vega. 'I think I should say sorry to you, too,' she said in a moment of seriousness. 'It's so clear that you loved Susannah as much as I did, and I can't blame you for what happened.'

'I know you miss her,' Mr Vega said. 'But I hope that Ivy and Olivia can bring you back some of her joy, like they have for me.'

Rebecca had tears in her eyes. 'They already have. I should have said this days ago, but thank you for tracking me down.'

'I know it's what Susannah would have wanted,' Mr Vega replied.

'Finally!' Ivy said, relieved that her dad and her aunt could start to work things out.

Ivy and Olivia leaped up for a group hug. At last their dad and their aunt had found something in common.

Ivy grinned at Olivia through Rebecca's

hug, and Olivia, who was slowly being crushed by Mr Vega, beamed right back.

It was starting to feel like they had a full family at last.

TWIN TALK!

In this instalment of Georgia Huntingdon's all-access interviews with the twins, Ivy and Olivia talk about their journey to discover the non-vampire side of their family.

Georgia Huntingdon: What was it like to find out about your human relatives?

Ivy Vega: I have to be honest, it was a little weird. My whole life had been about getting used to being a vampire, and learning how to blend in with regular people. I knew my biological mother was human but, for some reason, I hadn't really thought much about that side of my family.

Georgia: Had your dad never mentioned that you had an aunt — your mom's twin sister?

Ivy: He had decided not to. He was already in enough trouble with the vamps higher-up for marrying a human — I can see why he made the choice that he did, to not involve my biological mom's family. He didn't like doing it, but I'm sure he was worried that there was a risk of too many non-vamps knowing *the secret*.

Georgia: So, does your aunt know now?

Ivy: No, she still doesn't.

Georgia: Are you sure your mom never told her she was in love with a vampire? Being one yourself, you know how much twins share with each other.

Ivy: I do, of course. But, believe me, if Aunt Rebecca knew that my dad was a vamp, she would have said something during that whole period when the two of them just *could not* get along.

Georgia: Do they really hate each other that much?

Ivy: Not now. In fact, I don't think they ever did *hate* each other. They were just never that close in the first place, and then . . . Mom died . . . and my dad decided to move away to raise me.

Georgia: How does it feel to keep that big a secret from such a close relative?

Ivy: Not very good, but secrecy is part of being a vampire in this world. Only a few 'bunnies' can handle knowing the truth. Like Olivia. If anything, having to keep the secret from Aunt Rebecca makes me appreciate the relationship I have with my sister even more.

Georgia: So, how was it, getting to know the other side of your family?

Ivy: It was . . . odd. After spending a few weekends on a ranch, I had an idea how Olivia must have felt trying to get used to Transylvania. I might as well have been green with long tentacles for arms, you know? Being out in the countryside, I felt like an actual alien. A scary alien, too.

Georgia: Why scary?

Ivy: Because I couldn't go near the horses on the farm without them totally freaking out. It was like they could sense my vampire-ness.

Georgia: Oh my gosh! How did you cover that up?

Ivy: Aunt Rebecca just assumed I wasn't a 'ranch' sort of girl. Which is actually totally true! I just wish I hadn't had to lose her favourite horse – my *mom's* favourite horse – in order to prove that.

Georgia: Ah yes, you had mentioned there was some drama at the ranch. But that all got sorted out, right?

Ivy: [nods] Eventually, yes. But it was a big, big disaster there for a second. A bigger disaster than Camilla casting Garrick as Olivia's romantic lead in the school play!

Georgia: Olivia and Garrick?!

Ivy: [shudders] Ugh! Can you imagine? But I'll let Olivia tell that story. Anyway . . . I had a crazy moment, trying to prove that I could belong at the ranch. Olivia had done so well adapting to life in Transylvania that I wanted to show I *could* fit in with the human side of our family just as well. But . . . it all went more wrong than the time I thought making onion ice cream sounded like a cool, unconventional idea.

Georgia: That must have been terrible.

Ivy: It was. If the taste of onion gets stuck in your mouth, you need industrial strength mouthwash to get it out.

Georgia: No, I meant . . . losing the horse. And not fitting in at the ranch.

Ivy: Oh! Right. Yes, it was horrible. I honestly don't think I've ever felt as bad in my whole life as I did that day. The horse was called Lucky, my mom's favourite. Of all the horses I could let run out of the stables, huh?

Georgia: You talk about having such a tough time at the stables but, as we know, you've returned many times since then. What brought about the turnaround in your opinion of the countryside?

Ivy: Finding my mom's journal was a big turning point for me. You see, my dad never spoke much about her. I don't like to pester him for information, as I can see that his heart is still broken, even now. But, every time he spoke about her, he always made her seem utterly perfect, popular – flawless. Aunt Rebecca was the same. But the journal was almost like Mom talking directly to me – and, in the journal, she was being completely honest. To find out that she didn't always feel confident, that she had a bit of the 'rebel' about her – that she wasn't always at home on the ranch . . . I needed to know that Mom occasionally felt like a bit of a misfit. It's nice to know that, even if I had been born a bunny, I'd probably be the same old Ivy. [Laughs]

Georgia: So, this crazy horse, then? How did you manage to bring it back to the ranch?

Ivy: [giggling] That was the power of singing! I read in Mom's journal that spooked horses calm down when they're sung to, so I tried 'I Wear my Sunglasses at Night'. Then Brendan showed up, and when I asked him to sing . . . the first thing that came to his mind was 'The Itsy Bitsy Spider'!

Georgia: That's adorable.

Ivy: [sighs] I know.

Georgia: Oooh, what is that look? You just got all wistful.

Ivy: I did?

Georgia: Yuh-huh. Is something wrong between you and your perfect boyfriend?

Ivy: No . . . no, not so far . . .

Georgia: What do you mean, *not so far?*

Ivy: That's another story . . . for another time.

Georgia: Gosh, how intriguing. Now, if I can turn to you for a moment, Olivia . . . Some people would not expect a cheerleader — a girly-girl — like yourself to be at home on a farm. But the truth is you actually loved it at your Aunt Rebecca's, right?

Olivia Abbott: Who knew there was a country girl inside me, waiting to burst out?

Georgia: 'Burst out'? The way I heard it, the country girl positively *cartwheeled* out.

Olivia: [laughs] I don't know about cartwheeling. Maybe she just did a little flip!

Georgia: What was it about the countryside that was so great for you?

Olivia: Probably the peace and quiet. You know, the tranquillity? After the chaos of Transylvania, it was nice to relax a little. I was also still a little frazzled from doing the movie with Jackson.

Georgia: You and Jackson were teaming up again to star in one of the most famous love stories of all.

Olivia: Not that we were the star-crossed lovers.

Georgia: Or should that be 'planet-crossed lovers'?

Olivia: [laughs] Ha! Yes, you're right. Only Camilla would dare to rewrite Shakespeare with aliens!

Georgia: The buzz is that she did it brilliantly.

Olivia: She so did . . . except for her casting.

Georgia: That's right. Your leading man ended up being someone quite . . . How can I put this?

Olivia: 'Horrid'?

Georgia: Well, I was going to go for 'unconventional' – but we can use your word!

Olivia: I'm sorry, that's mean of me. Even though I'm talking about Garrick Stevens. I was raised not to judge people on their looks – and I don't. It's just that . . . [shudders] Garrick actually seems to *like* smelling bad!

Georgia: But he must have been a good actor – to pip a *movie star* to the lead role?

Olivia: [grumble] It wasn't so much to do with his acting . . . Oh, gosh, I probably shouldn't tell you this.

Georgia: But now you've said that, you have to.

Olivia: Ivy was in a little bit of a spat with Garrick. She poured itching powder down his shirt to get back at him for putting it in her boots. When it was time for Garrick's audition, the itching powder just *happened* to make him act like a member of the alien race Camilla had imagined. So he got the part.

Georgia: And your dream scenario of sharing your first kiss with Jackson was almost ruined.

Olivia: Yes, my first kiss was almost with Garrick. *Ewwww* . . . Oh, uhm . . . [stammers] Not that I'm *Ewww*-ing because he's a vampire.

Georgia: You're *Ewww*-ing because he's a *smelly* vampire.

Olivia: Exactly!

Georgia: But everything worked out fine in the end. So . . . what's next for Olivia and Jackson?

Olivia: Well, I don't want to give too much away, but . . . it looks like there could be more projects in our future.

Georgia: That's so cool. You're practically a movie star now!

Olivia: Not quite.

Georgia: Just don't go all 'diva' on us once you become the biggest celebrity in the world.

Olivia: I promise, I won't!

Georgia: I'm sure Ivy wouldn't let you get a big head.

Olivia: Of course she wouldn't! That's why she's the best sister ever.

In the next part of Georgia's interview, she talks to the unlikely twins about their most recent experiences of fame and fortune – and their most dramatic identity mix-up EVER!

EGMONT PRESS: ETHICAL PUBLISHING

Egmont Press is about turning writers into successful authors and children into passionate readers – producing books that enrich and entertain. As a responsible children's publisher, we go even further, considering the world in which our consumers are growing up.

Safety First
Naturally, all of our books meet legal safety requirements. But we go further than this; every book with play value is tested to the highest standards – if it fails, it's back to the drawing-board.

Made Fairly
We are working to ensure that the workers involved in our supply chain – the people that make our books – are treated with fairness and respect.

Responsible Forestry
We are committed to ensuring all our papers come from environmentally and socially responsible forest sources.

**For more information, please visit our website at
www.egmont.co.uk/ethical**